THE SWIMMER IN THE DEEP BLUE DREAM

THE SWIMMER
IN THE DEEP BLUE
DREAM

SARA BERKELEY

RAVEN ARTS PRESS
Dublin

The Swimmer in the Deep Blue Dream
is first published in 1991 by
The Raven Arts Press
P.O.Box 1430
Finglas
Dublin 11
Ireland

ISBN 1 85186 092 4

Raven Arts Press receives financial assistance from The
Arts Council (An Chomhairle Ealaion), Dublin, Ireland.

Acknowledgments are made to the editors of *The
Sunday Tribune, Stet Magazine* and *The Irish Times* were
some of these stories first appeared.

Design by Rapid Productions. Cover design by Jon
Berkeley. Printed in Ireland by Colour Books
Ltd.,Baldoyle.

THE SWIMMER IN THE DEEP BLUE DREAM

For Steve

Contents

A Funny Thing To Do

My knuckle smarts where the skin has been grazed. When I washed my hands after cooking the meal it hurt suddenly. I grazed it myself this morning, on the wall of the lane that leads to the station. In a kind of wilful mood I dragged the hand behind me along the wall and the roughness made me drag it harder and still when I studied the graze on the train I saw it hadn't bled. There was dirt at the edges of the broken skin, that was all. Now it smarts, nagging.

On a Monday like this I had sat bone tired in this same chair. I had been up since four o'clock. We never got up at four, in fact by the time we got to bed it was often two or three and some nights we would still be reading at five, at that time when the night sounds are giving way to a kind of expectancy. Lou says you can train yourself to need less sleep. We both suffered a lot from this theory in the beginning, reaching that sort of tiredness where a blown fuse is a large event and you don't enjoy the taste of your food any more. But Lou doesn't change his mind very easily and so we experimented with sleep patterns in a more or less haphazard way until I came to the weary decision to sleep when I felt sleepy.

Still, it is only four months since I got up at four o'clock. Lou got up then too, silently shaved himself in the cold light of the kitchen, lit the gas with an anger I have only ever seen upon him at four in the morning or when something goes wrong with the car on the freeway. I was cowed, silenced. Not by anger, but by a mute kind of dread that I, in my turn, only ever experience very early in the morning. I hovered in the bedroom, unable to choose what to wear. I could not tell

9

Lou whether I wanted to drink tea or coffee. He poured me some grapefruit juice in a tumbler. We were still like that, angry and cowed, when we got into the car. Lou drives well and it relaxes him. That morning he drove racily, taking corners too fast and ignoring the ice on the roads.

"Lou it's still icy," I said.

"I know," he answered, almost happily. His anger was gone. He had simply driven away from it when we backed down the driveway and reversed into the street.

"We're going to sell the old house," he leaned across and put a hand on my knee. "Don't you be sad now."

I knew we were selling the house and I was very sad. As we drove, nostalgia began to replace my fear, and it was strangely comforting. We were about to do something very hard for both of us and yet, as we bowled along at an illegal speed, we began to feel spirited. Lou kept his hand on my knee.

"I *am* sad," I said, and as I did, I got a sudden urge to whistle.

We bought the house when we hadn't a penny. My brother Frank and Lou's father both looked it over for us and they both said we were mad. It was unsound, the plumbing was antiquated, the roof leaked. They both refused us money.

"This is typical" Frank said, "of your irresponsible attitude to life. You don't have a penny and you want to buy this house which needs thousands poured into it. You'll never have a penny. I won't give you money to throw away."

Frank is very fond of me. He and Alice see to it that Lou and I have some place to go when we lose our apartment; when our car breaks down he offers to rent us one till it is fixed. He lives in another state, otherwise he would drive us to work himself. I understood his refusal to give us money, but we had to have the house. We found the money with an aunt of Lou's, whose dead husband had amassed a fortune renovating old seaside houses just like this one. She saw the pictures and she spoke to her brother who left her in no doubt as to how dilapidated it was. She shook her head, and gave us the money.

"You children will never learn," she said. 'No one's going to teach you now except yourselves. You make a good job of this and when it's done I'll come and stay one weekend every year when the weather is hot."

We said we'd be happy to have her stay. In fact, all that spring we invited our friends to come and stay with us when the house was done. We invited people every time we met them. It became a kind of joke. I discussed with my girlfriends how I would make the place look, how the porch would be painted, where the cane chairs would go. They promised me scatter cushions and patchwork rugs. One Saturday Lou and I rescued an old sunken couch our doctor was throwing out. He helped us load it on a truck we borrowed for the day. He told us kindly he was glad to think we'd find some use for it. The couch became a kind of forlorn bastion in the empty sitting room. We positioned it where it would not suffer from the leaking roof and on autumn weekends we lovingly removed the small piles of leaves that blew in through the window's missing pane of glass and gathered in its corners. There were evenings we sat in that couch, smoking and planning the rehabilitation of the house around us. Sometimes when it was light and we still hadn't slept, we would go down to the beach and leave our clothes in a pile and run into the sea. From the water it seemed like the house was done. We planned the parties of friends we could have down at weekends, and we thought of special weekends when there would be just the two of us there. It never seemed that the time was very far away.

When Lou lost his job at the haulage firm we didn't go down to the house for a couple of months. It was winter anyhow and the winds on the coast are strong at that time of year. It wouldn't have been funny to feel the force of them as we bedded down in sleeping bags on the damp floors. People hinted that the house would have to go, but we kept up a mute resistance. It could wait. It would be there, waiting for us, when the summer came round again and things were looking up. The house was always there, never far from our

11

conversation, figuring squarely in our plans. While we had the house, the rest of the things would hold together. Lou couldn't find a job for some months. He would sit at a window, smoking and watching cloud patterns, or spend whole mornings in the local library reading the paper. That was a bad time and we tried to forget about it when March came and he began work with a glass company called Hayward and James. We began to talk of taking a trip down to see the house and we estimated to each other the amount of damage that might have been done over the winter. It was better than we expected. Some birds' nests, and a few broken window panes, that was all. The couch had been avalanched in leaves and as we cleared them off we sang our favourite Beatles songs. Lou would start one and I would join in where I found the words, and by the time it was over I would have the first line of another one ready to begin. We made a pact to spend two weekends in three down there doing the place up. Lou said he could get glass now to fix the windows. He was whistling a lot again.

It got warm and we did the first serious saving we had ever done and had the roof patched up by a man called Daney who lived around there. He said it was a fine view from our roof and if we ever felt like putting in a dormer room, we were to let him know.

"I have a brother does that kind of thing," he told us. "He'd be glad to do it for you."

He told us again what a fine view there was and when he had finished the job he said a dormer room would make the place a real home.

"You planning on living out here?" he asked us then. We said no, that we were city folk. The house was just for weekends, for holidays in the summer, for having friends down.

"It's like a hideout," Lou explained and the man said yes, that sometimes you needed a hideout.

With the roof sound we could take care of painting and putting some flooring in. We took care of one or two jobs over the weekends that Fall but interest rates were high and we began to miss payments on the dryer and the car. Frank invited us over there for Thanksgiving but we could never afford the flights and said we had other plans. The Fall was bitter. There was snow in September and we sold the dryer to get fuel. The house was draped in a constant web of damp clothes. Lou cursed as they brushed his head limply in the hall and as he fought angrily through them to the phone. We spoke rarely of our tiny house where the plaster littered the floors and the light fixtures hung raw from the ceilings. On November 3rd we couldn't meet the rent. The following weekend something happened in my head and I took the car and drove down there. I spent the night hunched in a corner of the sitting room, my eyes alternately fixed on the couch and closing in a sort of effortless sleep. In the morning I drove straight back and found Lou cutting wood in our back garden, something he did from time to time when he was feeling bad.

"I thought something awful might have happened," he said simply, and put his arms around me. "You're safe," he was saying, "you're back."

You come across things sometimes that should not be committed to paper. Years later when you are reading back over what you wrote of these things you wonder "what was I thinking of then?" and you lie awake at nights wondering about it. In the same way, there are certain things that should not be committed to speech. Lou put down his axe then and we cooked Virginia smoked ham and hash browns for breakfast. We ate in a kind of silence that could only be thinly hidden by the banter we always carried on with after times of great stress. The silence was very profound for both of us: I cannot say what Lou meant by his, for this is a thing you can never know about another person. Mine held sorrow because the hopes were dead; because Lou's father, Frank, the people who doubted were right. His aunt was right. The only ones who could teach us were eating ham and grits at our kitchen table.

Lou made bitter coffee and we looked at each other over our cups and smiled. It was hard to keep the smiles straight, they shook a little and my throat was tight. But Lou made the call to the agents at noon and we never discussed it. He never asked what made me drive down there or what I did. I never asked him how he knew we had to sell. I was sleeping a lot then and Lou began drinking gin. The agents made a date for 8 o'clock one Monday morning and we drove down in the ice. The house was looking sullen and betrayed. The roof with the fine view looked barren: it wanted a dormer to relieve the tiles. I could not quite bring myself to mention this to Lou, but we joked with the agent about the state of the place as though we'd never put an hour's work into it. Or a dollar bill, or a second's thought.

"You got a bad penny here alright," he looked at the crumbling porch and the tilting floors. "Some crook sold you a rotten egg."

"It's been a bit of a white elephant for us," Lou said, but the irony was lost on Myron P. Inglewood and we could hardly raise a smile ourselves. At last he was finished poking and measuring.

"We'll put it on the market Thursday," he said, as though we should be grateful. "You'll be lucky if it gets a song."

"We don't expect much," Lou said and shut the screen door hard. "It was a present from my aunt," he added in a funny voice.

I was tired all that Monday, and for many of the days that followed.

"I *was* sad, but now I'm glad we sold," I said to Lou. I said it more than once: to Frank and daddy and to most of my friends. I began going to bed earlier, sliding into a drugged kind of sleep while Lou sat in the kitchen with the paper and a glass. I bought a lot of books with the money set aside for paint and lightshades. I bought Tolstoy and Kurt Vonnegut and a complete collection of Proust. The books hunched, spineless, on the bookshelf Lou reluctantly put up. They hadn't the enthusiasm to be read.

I told Lou about this morning and my hand.

"Oh?" he said, still reading the football results. "How'd it happen?"

14

"I did it myself. I dragged it along the wall by the station."

"Hm?" he said, and scanned the last match. "Dragged what along the wall?"

"My hand." I held it out. He stared at it a moment, expressionless.

"Well, that was a bit of a funny thing to do," he said, and turned the page to baseball.

A Trip Out West

To get to his own front door, Hughie had to move eleven boxes of garden refuse. The hedge clippings had dried to skeletal sticks and the leaves underfoot crumpled scratchily when he trod on them. Hughie was a big man and that summer he had not been playing much tennis. He breathed heavily as he hauled the boxes up the short steep drive; he began to perspire and he was muttering to himself.

To open the door he had to fidget with the immense bunch of keys Kate had collected over 30 years. Some of these keys probably didn't open anything anywhere. They might have belonged to wardrobes Kate had sold to jumble sales, or to the cottages she owned on the coast that were never locked anyway. Hughie didn't know what most of them opened, and he muttered about this as he searched for the right one.

"All these keys," he grumbled, "Just like her. Bottle tops. Jars. She had to collect the lot. Bet they're all in here too." Finally he found the key and it turned stiffly in the lock. He stood in the hall and breathed the musty, closed-in air of a house that has been shut up for a long time. He had expected to feel overwhelmed at once by a familiar odour, or the sense of home he dimly remembered from childhood, but this did not happen. He wasn't sure exactly how it should feel, but he felt there ought to be something, some recognition. In the driveway, Kate's old Studebaker sat on its belly in the dust. She used to come and visit in that car when they still lived out west – pot-plants along the back window, old blankets on the seats. She hung a faded towel in the front windscreen to act as sunshield. Sheila used to complain: "Why can't she buy a regular cardboard one like everyone else? Safeway. Four dollars fifty. It wouldn't hurt."

Hughie blew dust off a photo of his parents that was on the hall stand. His mother's eyes squinted in the sun and there was the defiant uplift of the chin that was Kate's too. The photo frame left a gap in the dust and suddenly the whole place seemed to stare blearily at him from under a carpet of dust. Ten months of it clogged the house: he stopped in the door of the sitting room. He couldn't believe that such a short time could make the place look so bleak and uninhabited. The windows were thick with grime. Kate? She wasn't in this room. Not even her spirit was here. He touched the books on the shelves, ran a finger through the dust on the piano lid, but he did not touch any of the keys. The photos on the mantlepiece looked like anyone's family photographs: there he was, a fleshy scowling teenager, and Kate looking serious in spectacles, and Myron, the youngest, in the fork of a tree. He was there with Sheila and the kids – grouped awkwardly round the car on a family holiday, sunburned and grinning. Foolish, he looked, and he turned away ashamed.

Down in his studio on Redondo Beach, Marc Frostick was watching his girlfriend make a ballgown of the duvet. She held it around her naked body and strutted in what she imagined was a sexy fashion across the room and back.

"D'you know what'd be *really* erotic?" Marc said in slow, exaggerated tones. The telephone rang and he leaned from the beanbag, still grinning at her, to pick it up. "Hello, Marc Frostick?" His girlfriend wiggled her hips under the duvet. "Oh – hi dad!"

"IT'S MY DAD," he mouthed at her, with a kind of frenzied delight. She clapped both hands to her mouth to stifle a scream of laughter and the duvet dropped in a silent heap on the carpet.

"Well yeah, dad," he said soberly. "I'm kinda tied up all weekend here. Where ARE ya? Uh-huh, Kate's place. Right. Fresno." He covered the phone and mouthed "HE'S WEIRD!" The girlfriend burst into fresh

18

paroxysms of stifled laughter and sat down suddenly on the duvet.

"Well no, dad, I mean yeah, I got lots of schoolwork, y'know? I got summerschool finals in a week. Is mom there too? No? Tch. Look dad, I'd love to come up. It's just a bad time." He motioned to his girlfriend to put the duvet on again, and mouthed something indistinguishable. "Uh-huh. Yeah, I guess you will, dad...Did she? Yeah, I remember now. Aunt Kate was always collecting." The girl had the duvet round her neck now and was stalking slowly towards him, one bare leg showing. He put his hand over the mouthpiece – "She was WEIRD TOO!" – and the girl let out a little scream.

"Huh, I bet there is lots of it...Well, like I said dad, any other time, y'know? Ok dad, yeah, I'm workin' hard alright...ok..see yuh soon dad." He hung up, there was a moment of suspense, then the two of them indulged in a lengthy and painful bout of laughter which ended with them both on the floor, entangled in the duvet.

"No" gasped the boy, "D'you know what'd be REALLY SEXY though? A BALLGOWN WITH NOTHING UNDERNEATH IT !"

Hughie opened a jar of Kate's pickles at lunchtime. He'd brought food with him, bread, peanut butter, some tins of pork and beans. The onions were large and pellucid. Black peppers floated on the surface of the pickling fluid. Pickles keep forever, Hughie said to himself as he prised the jar open. Kate pickled everything, and what she couldn't pickle she cured or preserved or dried. There were shelves of food in her back larder – bottles and jars of stores she had laid by for winter, or guests...for what? Hughie wondered, gazing along the shelves. It was a pity to waste them, but there was a certain urgency to get the task underway and he began to search for plastic sacks. Halfway through the search, however, he came to a sort of stop. Hunched at the kitchen cabinet below the sink he left off searching for black sacks in the various places where Sheila always kept hers. It wasn't the search that seemed futile. It wasn't even the great task of clearing the house that had called for a week of his annual leave and a trip out west. Hughie was stopped in his tracks like a weighty animal, dimly aware that the light filtering down through the forest leaves was no longer enough. He was arrested by the notion that for some time now he had been blundering, muddling through. He struggled to put a name to the feeling. It had not only been with him since coming to Kate's, the oddly disquieting conversation with his son, his ill-equipped battle with the house that had belonged to his dead sister and was now, until he could sell it, his. Abruptly he stood. It had settled on him, the futility of trying to see clearly. Furrowing his brow as though to recollect something, he walked uncertainly to the timber door that opened on the cellar steps. In the cellar there was more food and the accumulations of thirty years. Hughie scarcely glanced about him. On the front wall was Kate's wine cellar. The racks held twenty, maybe thirty bottles of wine – home brewed and vintage alike. Kate had loved a good wine. But Hughie reached out and took the first bottle that came to hand. Not pausing even to examine the label, he went heavily back up the cellar steps to the kitchen.

Sheila Frostick was worried and annoyed. In her annoyance she dialled a wrong number and called the Dunkin' Donuts on third street before she got through to her eldest daughter.

"Carole? Is that you?" she snapped. "Is your father there?" Her daughter was tired and she didn't know where her father was. The kids were home from school, a jaundice scare. She hadn't seen her father for some weeks.

"Well he's disappeared then," said her mother shortly. "He's not been home for two days. No note. Not a sign."

Carole thought she remembered something about a trip out west. To Aunt Kate's house. There was a brief silence.

"Ah. Well. That's that then. Have you had the children seen by a doctor?"

No, Carole hadn't been in touch with the doctor yet, it was just a scare.

"That's what you have to do then. You don't want them on your hands for weeks, do you?"

No, Carole didn't want that. Hadn't Hughie said anything about going away?

"That's your father all over," Sheila answered grimly. "He probably didn't even pack clean underwear."

Hughie *had* packed clean underwear. His small shabby suitcase sat on a high bed in Kate's back bedroom. In it were six pairs of shorts and six pairs of threadbare grey socks. Hughie himself, his senses dulled by half a bottle of excellent wine, was in the larder, filling sacks with the contents of the shelves. He worked methodically, and his mind did not stray very far from the task that employed him. At six o'clock, he stopped work and ate half a dozen pickled onions, bread and cold beans, washed down with the rest of the wine. He slept a little in an armchair in the sitting room and when he woke it was getting dark. His head felt woolly and his movements were thick and clumsy. When he turned on the light, nothing happened. Kate's electricity supply had long been disconnected, with his own permission, given from New York. Now he stood in the centre of the darkening room and the emptiness of his heart bore down on him. It threatened to crush him with a terrible weight he could not understand or describe to himself. He gave a low groan. The streetlights flickered on, casting pale silver squares in the room, on the walls and on the bare boards. It was really quite a beautiful light. He turned to the black space of the doorway. He said his sister's name once, questioningly, but she did not appear. He lay down on the old stuffed sofa with the patchwork rug and pulled this about him, gripping his own body with his arms as though in the night he might freeze to death. He did not remove his shoes.

Chocolate Biscuits and Milk

"You're the stillest thing in the garden." This was my clear-eyed son, breaking out of the movement of his own playing to drop this observance coolly on my hot skin. The shock of his casual remark made me laugh at first. Then I caught all the movement in the garden with one turn of my head. There was plenty of it.

"Yes Nathan. I guess I am."

But he was already far away in some new fantasy, wanting to go inside to have tea "in five minutes", capering around a little, returning to where I was slipping back into the lethargy of sunbathing on the blanket, "is it five minutes yet?" and racing away again. By the time it was finally "five minutes", we were late. I got up too quickly and trailed blankets, mugs of cold tea and discarded cardigans dizzily into the kitchen where the lunch dishes were sulking murkily in the sink.

"A boiled egg for Nathan, a boiled egg for Ruthie, a boiled egg for Anthony," I recited as I hurried through the preparations for a scanty tea.

"No, I don't want a boiled egg," Nathan decided from the corner where he had been eating the sugar. "I want roasted chicken." But even the eggs were underdone in the hurry and my children were startled into eating alone while I searched for things I wanted to bring with me. The edge of panic had scarcely worn off my impatience when Ruth and I finally turned the corner in the village and saw the bus bulked reassuringly in the road, throbbing hotly over the oil spillages, giving a sigh of the automatic doors as they snapped lazily behind us. It was a relief to have caught it, but it was sweet relief to be the last on and I leaned forward almost lovingly as she lumbered steeply round the corner, as though I were sharing a private joke with her when she threatened to tip us back down the stairs.

It was a halcyon busride; Ruth, small like a young sister beside me. I looked at her once, telling me animatedly about the trouble her friends were always getting into at school (she was never involved), and reminded myself wordlessly, as so often before, she is your child. Your child. Keep her there.

The city was lazing, sundrenched, secure in the evening having drunk its fill of sunshine all day. It was replete. The suburbs winked of car doors closing and the corners where the bus nuzzled up were rounded and slipped easily by. Warmth everywhere. I looked at the sun-tops and shorts, scanning the women of my own age for what looked best. Dress your age, darling, Arthur would tell me. If you want people to treat you like a mother of three, you've got to dress like one. Arthur always missed the point. It was precisely because I didn't want people to treat me like a mother-of-three that I still dressed like a student.

There was a gross woman in tartan trousers on St. Stephen's Green.

"You see that woman?" I pointed her out to Ruth. "I bet she's American."

"Yeah, they always have tartan trousers," she said matter-of-factly, as though insulted I had interrupted her with such an obvious remark. You've got to get a balance right, I reminded myself humbly. You've got to presume knowledge and work backwards – that way they won't feel patronised and they won't lose patience with you and move on. You won't lose patience with me and move on, I begged my daughter silently as we descended for our stop.

I suddenly needed an excuse to bring her down to the University. We had plenty of time, the bus had been quick, and I just needed to walk through the place for a bit. She came, neither willingly nor unwillingly, and I felt curiously ashamed needing to walk around there, choking back the bitter fusion of pride and nostalgia, trying to be casual as I showed her things. We stood in Fellow's Square and she was silent, in a mood I could not fathom, so that I risked a lot venturing to say

"This is where daddy and I kissed each other for the very first time."

This time I had not once imagined seeing him turn the corner at the library or raise his head from a book through a window somewhere. I was glad I had stopped imagining that. But I did want, suddenly and sharply, his large loose hug coming from behind as a surprise I wasn't supposed to flinch at. I did need his voice saying gruffly "How's that?"

Ruth slipped unexpectedly into my mood and I felt gratified and rather touched answering the questions she had asked many times before.

"And did you ever used to bunk off lectures to go places with him?"

"Mm. Sometimes."

"And did you tell the professors and things when you got engaged?"

It was just like I'd imagined it on the bus, showing her these things.

"And did daddy wear one of those cloak things?"

"Yes. He looked very fine in it. Come on – I can't be late for this talk."

As we left the University and walked to the library where I was to give a talk on Structure in the Modernist Poets, I could picture very clearly my younger son going to bed. The closer we got to the library, the more vividly I could see him. All the bedtimes of the last week or so merged in my mind in a collage of heavy-lashed eyes and arms held high to receive pyjama sleeves. There was the night he padded wet-eyed into the sitting-room, his voice edging darkly over into sobs as he told me of the ghost in his bedroom; and the night I sat with him, reading a novel until, when I thought he was asleep, he sat up with perfect composure and said in a sprightly voice

"You can go now mummy."

"I hope Anthony has put Nathan to bed," I said, as we mounted the steps of the library, and my voice was fringed with despair.

"It is asking a lot of today's critic to categorise Hopkins

as a Modernist." The used-up phrases bounced and jerked around in my head as we rode home on the last bus, the city discharging us gratefully into the countryside as though we had been keeping her from settling down for the night. I was feeling extraordinarily competent and full of iron resolutions after giving my talk. My hastily constructed arguments noted down while I was ironing, dropping Nathan to school, bringing Anthony swimming, had been well received. Perhaps the fire of a little humour added in the panic of the last few minutes before I spoke had helped warm the audience to me. I usually found a little spice to sprinkle on the dish before I served. Annoyed, I caught myself forming this neat little domestic metaphor. You are becoming mummified, I warned myself. Break out. Have a serious loss of dignity, for God's sake, or you'll ossify.

The house was sitting contentedly on its small hill – two lights inviting us up the driveway. Unhappily, one of them was Nathan's, which considerably narrowed the chances of him being asleep. He was not. In fact he was a great deal more wakeful than either Ruth or I.

"Mummy, won't you stay here until I'm asleep? And then before you go to bed, will you come in case I'm awake and sit with me again?"

"Yes Nathan." I sank gratefully onto his bed and eased off my shoes. He watched me solemnly, full-eyed. "Yes, I will." I kissed him. "I'll sit with you always."

In the morning I was at my typewriter on the kitchen table before the kids came down for breakfast. When they arrived, they ate over the typing, preoccupied in their own particular morning reticence, collecting sandwiches and busfares with a cold sort of automation, scarcely including anything more than my existence in their parting words. I typed on, frowning to try and circumvent a lonely sort of hole their morning routine always left in the pit of my stomach. The keys felt solid under my fingers and, as the awareness of Nathan, ready to be brought to school, grew in the background, I began to warm to my subject.

"Mummy, I'll hide and you come and find me."

"I see you Nathan, you're behind the fridge," I said firmly. I couldn't play hide-and-seek *and* type out my talk.

"Where?" came the muffled reply from behind the fridge. It was five minutes after the time we normally left the house.

"Have you got your sandwiches? Get your sandwiches." I prolonged the moment of leaving as much as possible. The argument I had come upon was a winner. I couldn't let it go.

"I can't. I'm hiding."

"And an apple. It's in the fridge you're behind."

Behind which you are. Even if Arthur had opened the back door and corrected me as he always did, the sound of the latch would have been drowned out by the depression of one of the keys. Perhaps the M key. Or the Q. Then the keys would remain motionless, although it did not seem unlikely that some of them may have continued tapping on their own for a moment or two into the silence. Nathan emerged from hiding. There was an old piece of bacon rind stuck to his shoe.

"MummyI'mgoingtobelatefor SCHOO-EL!!"

I typed the last word of my sentence. The letters printed themselves with a sickly kind of sound on the paper, not at all the familiar, reassuring clack. I briefly scanned the typed page. In a romantic novel, I – the lovestruck and forsaken heroine – would find my lover's name typed absently in the middle somewhere.

"But then romantic novels wouldn't have typewriters in them, or little boys with bacon stuck to their shoes, would they?" I said to Nathan and he piped a decisive "No!" as we left the house, late, unbuttoned, gloriously undone.

Alone, I tested out my voice in the still kitchen -

"I AM A MOTHER OF..."

but the words froze a little and seemed too grand, too all-encompassing, too dismissive for the jumble of plates and chipped mugs and half-sets of cutlery that made up my kitchen. Even the clock was the 'Free Gift' in some brochure from which I'd had the courage to choose some underwear for the boys. I am a mother of all this, I thought. Of the rattly windows and the ill-fitting door; of somebody else's sink. And I can drown out all the rattles and the stains with the indecent cackle of a typewriter, dredging up knowledge and ideas sown in student days, but the putty will stay chipped and the dribbles of tea will dry down the sides of the cups and I will not be one bit closer to being a mother of three than I was the day my fingers closed around a roll of white parchment and the cameras shuttered their mechanical eyes to imprison my graduate smile. Yet I had served my apprenticeship. It had seemed natural to graduate into the marriage bond with Arthur; to bring about the children whose shadowy, half-imagined figures had filled college evenings over pints in the bar. Three terms of pregnancy, three stretches of feeding, child-shattered nights, teething. The phases cluttered the floor of the last ten years like so many wrappers crumpled from long-forgotten gifts. And now Ruthie sometimes woke in the might and thought she saw her father's face moulded out of the bumps in the wallpaper. I rarely dreamed of Arthur, though dreams often spread themselves out over the whole night and I would wake with the feeling of having been through a lot in them. More vivid were the daylight dreams. I would write down the way I had seen him and put the writing away, glad to have written it, knowing it would not happen.

I let the morning stretch and bend a mechanical arm – made beds, washed up and left the house to shop. It was sunny, but I still felt as though I would throw no shadow. Sometimes, as this morning, I could get mute comfort from watching peoples' faces, when they were kind and intelligent. In the shopping centre, I went down the escalator behind a woman with an oldish man I guessed was her father, and her two children. The young boy ran on down the escalator and stayed at the end, running madly on the last two stairs and calling up
"I love this! I love doing this!"
"Christopher! Don't do that!" his grandfather called,

but the boy didn't hear. "He'll hurt himself," he remonstrated feebly to his daughter, but she was humming and simply kissed his upturned forehead with a smile.

"Mummy, what's the name of that thing you're humming?" the daughter asked. They had just reached the bottom and the mother was preoccupied with clothes in a shop window. "It's the Sorcerer's Apprentice," I wanted to say. "Die Zauberlehrling." But I bit it back. I bit it back and turned away from them. One must not intrude on other peoples' worlds, I told myself, and picked a trolley to wheel numbly round the supermarket.

Back home, the time Nathan finished school sat placidly across the table from me as I typed my lecture. I thought that with half an hour to go it seemed to fold its arms and assume a smug expression. I knew it was not to be moved.

"Alright!" I snapped with five minutes to go. "You win. But I'll get this paragraph done."

It always won. My only revenge was Nathan's bedtime, which approached wearily and sometimes balked at the threshold, but always dragged the quiet balance of the evening at its heels. As I typed the last paragraph, my imagination veered off a little into a scene where I sat typing at the kitchen table past the time where Nathan was to be collected from school. I sat until the angry little figure got up, its arms hanging uselessly at its sides and left the table, passing out the back door, screaming thinly and wordlessly of its betrayal. Imagine if I didn't collect Nathan from school. Imagine if I didn't cook a dinner, or drive Anthony to the swimming pool. Imagine if I didn't do any of these things; if I didn't do anything.

"But you've no alternative. So you shouldn't be opening the Big and Silent Doors to the Unattainable." Arthur's words eddied round the typewriter and wreathed the kitchen chairs. Our Big and Silent Doors that we had opened wide so many times; somehow it didn't seem permissible to approach them any more, even with mere curiosity. Perhaps because the

Unattainable really was what it said it was, and no longer simply a state we regarded as within our eventual grasp. Perhaps because I was a mother of three.

I removed the sheet from the typewriter and slipped my shoes on under the table. Nathan would be waiting, surveying the clutch of mothers with the complacency of a child who knows he will be collected. I thought how his entry through the gate at nine plunged him into complete unawareness of life outside, of my own morning, shopping, typing, cooking things. Until I surfaced, struggling, at the school door at half past one, I might have ceased to exist for a few hours. And for my part – should I not feel shame and guilt and wish to make it up to my young son that I had wrestled with doubt over my role to him? Instead I seemed to come back into it as soon as I saw the school roof, as you slip into an old dress you have loved very much. Seeing his intent head through the classroom window, I even smiled one of those satiated smiles and felt I had come upon a rare moment of his unawareness, by chance, as one does some of the finest things there are.

As he came out, preoccupied with getting both arms into one sleeve of his coat and saying goodbye to his friends, I tried to pretend he was someone else's child and look at him in that light. Were his trousers not a little short? And the schoolbag, an old one of Anthony's – didn't all the other kids have new ones? I silently resolved to get one of those Thomas the Tank Engine schoolbags in Woolworth's, and increased my enthusiasm over the paper flowers he'd been making all morning.

"One for you, and one for Ruth, and one for Anthony...mummy?"

"Mm?"

"Will Daddy mind if I don't have a flower for him?"

"I shouldn't think so Nathan."

And perhaps he could do with some new shoes as well. In fact, when the cheque came through for the talk, I would get something for all of them. Something they'd really like. Perhaps it would stretch to a trip to the country, a day in the zoo. The phone bill could wait. The man in the washing machine shop might let me pay two months' installments next month. It would work out.

"Maybe I'll make him another one," I heard Nathan murmur as we turned up the garden path. "For the next time when I see him."

"You do that son. Paper flowers don't die like ordinary ones. They go on and on." And on and on. Nathan was already immersed in the world of a small insect making its way across our front doorstep. He crouched on his hunkers peering at it, all thoughts of paper flowers gone. It would never get made. But then, it would never be collected. I shut the door after Nathan who had squashed the creature with his thumb, and we began to sing the song we always sang after school when it was time for our chocolate biscuits and milk.

End of the Line

We pull into the leafy drive of a wooden house. Marilyn shuts the engine off and reaches down for her bag. I stare ahead at the house.

"Come on. We'll go in now. There's no one there. We can make some coffee and you can tell me everything."

Our feet crunch on the gravel. Always feet crunching on gravel, you can tell it's my story when you hear that because I love the sound. It has a purpose and it makes me think of my feet, which I like. The house looks reassuring and I want to be inside, to walk right through and out the back, and in again. Marilyn opens the front door and leads me through the dim hall and down a passage, out the back to a porch, glassed in, looking out on the garden. The house smells of cinnamon. My head is loosening – the fog is clearing for the first time in the story. It is Marilyn's house that is doing this.

The porch is warm and full of easy chairs and an old faded red couch that looks as if you can sink deeply into it. She leads me to the couch and sits me down. She's taking off her coat and scarf.

"I'll make some coffee."

She's so bright and cheerful and I have been compliant, allowing her to lead me and make the arrangements; it's been easy to follow her, always heading towards something, somewhere private where we will be able to sit down and talk. But now we're here I don't want it. I want to wander round her house, look at the things she has, savour being here for the first time. You are only once in a place for the first time and the whole thing is decided then.

She's going to bring the coffee cups in and we still

have to sit down and talk. Already I want to come in through the hall, for the first time, again. But the whole thing has begun; the bloom is gone and it is no longer fresh. There is even the faint sickening squeal of cogs turning – a machine I myself have set in motion. There's no stopping it. I want to climb the stairs, the gloom of an upper landing and the sealed quiet of the bedrooms. Rooms you can only imagine always seem enormous. Warm corridors up there, thick pile carpets, giant shadowy bedrooms: Marilyn's bedroom, its door ajar. A dressing table, the powders, the bottles of scent, a wardrobe, huge and polished, hiding the still forms of her clothes: skirts, shirts...a fur? Suddenly the couch seems red hot and I jump up hurriedly and stand in the doorway to the kitchen.

"Marilyn – uh – where's your bathroom?"

"Oh, right through here." She smiles brightly. She's leading me again, down the hallway and to the right, where a room of books is visible through a doorway, and beyond it she motions to another door. My legs are like jelly. I lock the door behind me and listen to her footsteps returning to the kitchen. The water will be almost boiled. Boiling water spilling into the cups, the churning of grounds. Cookies, the moist, chewy type with the raisins and oats – "Almost Home" they're called.

"Almost home," I groan, before I'm sick in the sink.

After a little while I look around the bathroom. It's not the type where the toilet paper matches the toothbrush mugs. Yet it's obviously not a family but a guest bathroom. Tiny. No windows. The towels sit straight on the rail. I feel pretty safe in there. When I've stopped trembling so violently I reluctantly unlock the door and return slowly to the kitchen. The book room has a bluish tinge. All those film books. Marilyn, can I look at your books? Could I just go in there, close the door – just look at the titles? Is there a window in there, onto the front lawn...

She is sitting in an easy chair, glasses on, reading the paper. The glasses give me a fright. The coffee's on a small table, steaming offensively. No cookies, though.

"Alright?" she folds the paper. She's looking over the glasses, like I was afraid she would.

"Marilyn, I know I keep saying things that don't make sense," I say thickly, the spaces between my words seeming uneven. "I hear them afterwards and I don't know why I've said them." Blood heats my cheeks.

"I know that." Yesterday all I wanted was to hear a voice like this, kind, reassuring. "It's alright. Just sit down and tell me what's going on."

I look around the room desperately. "Couldn't we go somewhere else?"

For a moment she looks bewildered, then she sighs and looks down at her fingers which she has spread out as though to relinquish something.

"I think this room is best."

I'm sick! I'm sick and no-one will believe! There's nothing wrong...no! I'm sick! Those blanks. The fog. The dreaming.

My heart pounding, I cross to the couch and sit down.

"I was sick," I say dully. Anything to postpone the moment when I have to start. Her silence. My words. Hideous! How long before I have to try and put words on...nothing? My brain is trying for a slippery hold on something – a reason why I might have brought things to this pass, a story of what might have happened to someone, that would have Marilyn shaking her head in disbelief and sympathy; telling me not to worry, it's over now, I'm with a friend...There's been quite a long pause.

"I wake up in the street," I mumble. With the words, the blood begins to leave my head. It's happening again, the old familiar blackness, the swirling. My eyes prickle. "I think I might be going to faint."

That's what I want! A scene rehearsed a hundred times: waking on hard white tiles, faces looming kindly over me – "You fainted" – but the picture fades there. There's nothing after, but the vague possibility of being looked after. Someone's house. A warm room.

"Put your head between your knees." Marilyn is all efficiency. She moves the coffee table and gently pushes my head down until I'm in that humiliating position; memories of church, of standing in the school choir, the air getting thinner and hotter, the crush getting greater. Still, the blood is sweet, returning in the nick of time like this, and as I start to feel better I also start to feel absurd and – not now! – stupidly like laughing. That's right, blow the whole thing why don't you.

I sit up, shrugging Marilyn's hand away.

"Would you like a drink of water?"

"No thanks." It is clear to me suddenly, brilliantly clear, the route to the front door, the short gravel drive, curving mercifully out of view, and out on the road – could I flag a lift? A bus? But first, a concentrated effort to think of something Marilyn might have to fetch from upstairs. "Do you have any...sweets?"

"Sweets?"

"You know – glucose. Pastilles. I just need something sweet. Throat lozenges would do."

"Yes. Yes, I have some – I think," she checks herself, rising from the couch and looks at me, "You'll be ok?"

I nod. "Thanks Marilyn." Of course I'll be ok. It always returns, this self-preservatory instinct. Just when the height is making my head spin deliciously and I want to GO, it steps in and hauls me back from the edge, with the violence of love. Again I want to laugh, but not with mirth, and anyway there isn't time. A surge of adrenalin proves that my body has already decided what my mind is not yet sure about: GO! Through the door and down the passage, blue rooms on either side and the dim hall ahead – my brain is panicking, a smart struggle between the need to escape and the shock of leaving so rudely this house where I came for help.

It would be nice to skip ahead, to pick the story up ten merciful miles down the road and skip the hot, befuddled details of my flight. A flashback, perhaps, idly mentioning the leaving of her house, the car, the bus I luckily caught right across the road...but I'm here, I'm at the front door, trying to turn the handle without making any noise, I'm on the gravel now, remember the gravel? How I loved the sound of it not twenty, not fifteen minutes ago? I hate it now, the scrunching sound it makes, I loathe it with a mixture of fear and

revulsion as I near the curve and hear her call me –
once! twice! – in needle-sharp treble. *Don't look back!*
My jogging accelerates to a full sprint, round the bend,
through the gates and onto the placid suburban street.
All is panic now. Where can I hide? Terrible physical
anxiety that she will follow and catch up. My body
responds with jerky, stricken movements, I start off to
the left, then remember we came from the right. A bus
stop – was there a bus stop? I can't think, can't
remember the road, it was a maze of suburban
turnings, side streets, junctions, little hills, where's the
main road? She'll follow! She'll get in the car and come
after me, WHAT WILL I SAY?

The bathroom, it must have been in the front, she saw
me out the window. Pounding at full speed down the
pavement, I'm beginning to get dizzy again, but there's a
hard little voice in my inner ear: the one who made me
want to laugh, the one who told me "GO!" It's alright,
the voice is saying, with a kind of cruel triumph, keep
going. You won't faint. You're not allowed to now. And
she won't find you. She's not allowed to either.

It's there, the main road, it's right ahead, and if I keep
running full tilt like this down the slope, I'll career right
onto it and that will be the end of everything. I'm almost
shouting with the pain in my chest and legs now and
I'm laughing too. Go on, says the voice – harder now,
louder – just do it! Go on! You know you can't! But I
can. Gasping and laughing, I veer round onto the main
road and dash straight across and round the front of
the bus whose doors are just snapping shut with a
wheeze. I shout "Hey! Hey!" and am pounding on the
doors even as they swing lazily open again. "Alright,
alright lady," the driver says reprovingly and I scramble
up the steps. A bus! A bus! As it pulls away I'm lurching
drunkenly down the aisle clutching my ticket, gasping
and fighting for breath – and laughing. I drop into a
seat and rest my head against the shuddering window.
A bus. I'm travelling. I got away.

Now is the time for mercy. *This* is where I, the camera-
man, take pity on the figure in the bus and draw back

from her tortured drive. The story is over. A pitch was reached and the descent is no-one's territory but hers. Marilyn won't catch up with her. No one will find her. No one is looking. A few passersby notice her standing outside the shoe-shop where she alighted from the bus. She's not laughing any more. She's looking odd, in fact, standing like that in the middle of the pavement, looking at nothing. People have to walk around her. Some of them glance at her curiously, but only the kids stare.

If we are discreet, it will be possible to follow her, when, after ten minutes, she moves towards the subway; down, through the ticket barriers and on down to the platforms. Here again, she seems to stand alone in her own space, not waiting on either platform, not leaning against a wall, not sitting on a bench. Not even, apparently, waiting. But when a train comes she gets on and sits at the end of the carriage, next to the window. The train begins to move and she's crying now, quietly, almost unnoticeably. It is possible to sit on a train, in broad daylight, with your face uncovered, and weep without anyone asking you why. It is possible to get on a train with no destination in mind. You can ride to the terminus. Only then, finally, will a guard gently tell you it's the end of the line. And maybe, if he's a kind man with kids of his own, he'll notice the tears and ask you if you're alright. But if you mumble something in reply, if you stand and mumble something and walk right past him to the open door – what can he do?

Happy Birthday Mr. Keyes

Harry lost Matthew Stone just three days before his 50th birthday. He holed up in his study, shuffling through reams of paper covered in his own close scrawl, looking for clues. He sat there all night and the study window was open and he caught a cold. On the morning of his birthday he decided that Matthew, tall, silent and just a little too self-assured, was not coming back.

"Darling what are you doing?" his wife said from the bathroom doorway.

"I'm shaving my beard off, Kate," Harry said quietly.

After thirty years of hiding behind a beard, his chin recoiled in shock from its nakedness in the mirror. I am not a young man anymore, Harry thought bitterly, my nose is stuffed, and now Matthew leaves without a trace.

"But darling," Kate said, and suppressed mirth made her suck her cheeks inward, "your chin! I've never seen it before!"

Harry swung round. His heart was full, his throat was sore, and in his anguish he forgot that he had shaving foam in his ears.

"Kate-" he said in a choked voice.

Kate took her husband to the kitchen and sat him at the table. She poured him a cup of coffee and made him some toast he didn't want.

"Now. Tell me. It's Matthew, isn't it?"

"He's gone, Kate."

"No he's not."

Fine, thought Harry. I tell my wife blue is blue and she says no.

"I can't find him," he corrected, humbly.

"He's around, as sure as I am, or Nick or Laura, or

any of the other people who love you."

"Hey dad!" said his son, passing through the kitchen, "The big 5-0, huh?" He paused at the back door. "Dad," he said, "you've only got half a beard."

Harry looked from his son to his wife. Kind, affectionate, even loving, they were laughing at him. The moment struck them both as the funniest thing that had happened in weeks, they looked at one another and exploded into laughter. His son laughed the same way as Kate: long, sobbing breaths, his head thrown back. He was still laughing as he roared off on his bike, and Kate was dabbing her eyes at the breakfast table.

"I'm sorry, Harry, really."

"That's alright." He fingered his itchy chin thoughtfully. "I'm not concentrating properly. I've wasted so much time and it has come to nothing." I shouldn't bother, he was thinking. All this trouble. Kate has other things on her mind.

"Why don't you try the train?"

"Hm?"

"Try riding the train – what time was it he took?"

"The 3.16. The 3.16 from Waterloo to Burgess Hill." Except he didn't get off at Burgess Hill. He stayed on the train until it reached Brighton. Harry looked at his wife and smiled, happily, for the first time in his fifty-first year.

Later in the morning, he drove to his daughter's house on the other side of town. Laura said he looked like a boy without his beard.

"It's taken twenty years off you dad!" she laughed her pretty laugh. The Keyes laugh.

"Not grandad," said his three year old grandson stubbornly, and refused to sit on his knee. They talked of his childhood and hers, as they always did on birthdays; of the countryside where they had lived before coming to London, the flat land that even in drought or snow had its faces, the snow ruts, the sand rut of a mouth, the drift or bluff of a nose. The child crouched on his hunkers, colouring the world with his crayons. At noon, Harry rose to go. Laura pressed him to stay for lunch but he smiled and shook his head.

"I'm taking a train ride this afternoon."

"Oh dad – reduced rates don't start till you're SIXTY!"

"I'm practising." He kissed his daughter and stood in the doorway. Laura nodded, amused.

"It's alright baby," she reassured her son, who was tugging at her skirt. "It's still grandad. Still the same crazy old butterfly chaser."

Harry was on the 3.16 when it pulled out of Waterloo, as Matthew would have been. He made quick jottings in the notebook on his knee, things his boy would notice, the London he would see as it shunted by. The thick paper wad was safe in the briefcase, tight black leather, on the rack overhead. The train passed Elephant and Castle and he nodded inwardly, ticking off the first landmark, and his heart brimmed with quick delight in the name. The London names – Angel, Burnt Oak, Harrow-on-the-Hill; like Indian names, the whole of England was a landscape of them – Saltfleet, Blackpool, Wells Next The Sea. Stone. There was a place called Stone in Staffordshire. It was a smooth name, pale and dark like his boy. Hardly a boy, though; where do the thirties come? Somewhere in between. About the age of the young man who had taken a seat opposite, by the door, twitching at the trousers of his dark suit as he sat down and crossing his legs assuredly. Harry saw that he had no luggage. The river, he jotted, noticing as he did the way the veins stood up on the back of his hand, like he was gripping the pen very tightly. As a young man, you had to grip things quite tightly before the veins pronounced themselves like that. The river is very close, he wrote. Matthew senses things like that. Out of the corner of his eye he noticed the young man yawn and rest his head back and he permitted himself a glance. Dark hair, long lashes over the closed eyes, impeccably dressed in the dark suit and white shirt. Harry smiled, secretly amused. Makes it all the easier, he thought. Now I can see how Matthew would sit here, composed as always – cool as a cucumber, my boy – though in this heat he'd never let the suit bother him, always remove the jacket.

41

As he was forming the thought, the lad opened his eyes and began carefully removing his jacket. He folded it on the seat beside him, and, as he did so, caught Harry's eye. As the older man looked away, he thought he caught the glimmer of a smile on the boy's face. The stations passed, sleepy towns, ambling country villages, the afternoon unfocussing the colours; Harry ticked the names off and, almost against his will, began to play a game with himself. Matthew, sitting opposite in shirt and dark trousers, must find the carriage too warm for even a tie. What if – Harry concentrated his gaze on the top button of the white shirt, and as he did, the boy's hand came up and slowly, without him opening his eyes, eased the button open and loosened the tie.

Harry turned his eyes abruptly away and stared out the window. A slight flush troubled his cheeks and neck. He felt a desire to laugh, but at the same time wished he was sitting at home in his study, writing in black ink on cool white sheets. This train journey, this whole idea had been excessive. There was no need to take things to extremes. His head felt tight and hot. He'd been a fool to waste his birthday in this way. In his sudden agitation, he discovered he had closed his notebook. He stared down at the cover for a moment: Bovril, it said, prevents that sinking feeling. There was a picture of a man in pyjamas, riding a choppy sea on a giant bovril jar. He was grinning foolishly.

Well I *am* a sorry old fool, thought Harry. It's hardly a failure of imagination I'm suffering from. More like an overdose. And I'm missing the sights. I've already lost vital moments, missed the details Matthew would have caught. They were crossing the North Downs. Harry took in the colours, Laurie Lee's rolling tidal landscape, but he found it peculiarly tempting to steal another glance at his travelling companion. And, having glanced, and let his eyes rest longer than they should have on the tiny cleft in the chin, the smooth line of the cheek, he began to play the game again, half mockingly, half in earnest. It helps after all, he thought, defending himself against the rational impulse to forget the whole idea. Matthew, dreaming to the train's rhythm, moved a hand slightly and Harry knew he was thinking of the girl. They were about halfway to Brighton now and he must surely be aware of the train speeding south and gaining on the village where she lived. Burgess Hill. Harry thoughtfully drew a line beneath the name on his list. She was the real reason he had let Matthew slip from him, he reflected. It had been a mistake, letting her in like that, letting her get such a hold. I didn't even want her in there, he thought, she was a pawn, a distraction. As she took over, Matthew began to fade. The picture wasn't sharp any more. He glanced, to reassure himself, at the boy, but found to his confusion that the dark eyes were waiting to meet his. This time the boy smiled and inclined his head and Harry was forced to smile politely back, though he cursed himself for his indiscretion.

"The Weald," said Matthew, with a nod towards the window.

"I beg your pardon?" said Harry.

"The Weald. That's what they call those hills out there. Pretty, aren't they?" His voice was thin, almost like a boy's, not at all the rich bass Harry had imagined. It sounded as though it had hardly broken and gave him a quality of boyishness Harry suddenly found quite powerful. Of course, he *was* that contradiction of man and boy; he had been a success in his ten years of business, he carried an aura of confidence, and yet this note of uncertainty was exactly what was required to make the picture complete. Matthew was. He lived.

"Yes, they are." Harry never took his eyes from the boy's face. "I love this part of the country. Are you – from round here?"

"London." Of course he was from London. He lived in Wimbledon. Replingham Road. Red door, number 17.

"Are you..." But it was preposterous! Harry felt his heart contract. He was taking a game too far. Of course the boy was going to Brighton. Forty-nine of the fifty people on the train were going to Brighton. It was the only decent sized town on the line. "...on holiday?" he finished lamely, feeling his palms grow damp.

"Sort of." The boy smiled. It was conspiratorial, the

smile of a lover. Harry averted his eyes abruptly for the second time on the journey. Stop it, he told his heart. He felt his knees tremble, his beard stir darkly at the roots.

They were pulling into Haywards Heath, the stop before Burgess Hill. Harold Edmund Walter Keyes, he thought, leaning on all his names to steady himself, you are point five of a century old. This boy is a young Londoner on his way to Brighton. He is not Matthew. He is not yours. He will not alight at -

The boy was looking at his watch and Harry felt a kick of panic. He will *not* alight at Burgess Hill. It shall not be that way. But the girl! Jane! She had such power. She had begun to dominate as soon as Matthew met her, and now he had jumped on the 3.16 from Waterloo to answer her call. She had phoned, Harry had the conversation word for word in his briefcase, and she had begged Matthew to follow her south. Harry was aware what a thin line the boy trod, getting on that train. He only had to be strong at the right moment, to stay on the train for Brighton, and the girl would let go. The whole Jane episode would recede and he would be alone with his boy, sitting on a train, bound for Brighton. It was the vital change of mind. A book had a still point to its turning world, a point where the dance was. Harry knew that as soon as Matthew reached Brighton he would know what to do with him. He could have tea on the Front, take his leisure, mark time until the next train back up to London. But he must stay on the train now! Harry turned to the boy, as though to appeal to him. The same half-smile, slightly uneven lower teeth – why hadn't he noticed before? Matthew always seemed so physically perfect, yet that in itself was a flaw, unreal. "Teeth", he jotted in his notebook under Burgess Hill, "bottom centre, slightly uneven". It was amazing how clear it all was: he had known his boy imperfectly. The focus was sharpening now. The brakes began to screech, and as the sound grew, a noise in Harry's ears climbed above it. Matthew had risen, was picking his jacket up. Harry half rose too, panic locking his limbs.

"Matthew!" It was a cry, an old man's wail above the screaming brakes. Matthew's hand was on the door, he was down the corridor with the older man behind him, struggling to keep his balance as the braking threw him forwards, calling out "Wait! Matthew, wait! You can't -"

It wasn't until the boy had swung himself down to the platform and turned to look up that Harry saw the briefcase in his hand, raised a little for him to see, and he could no longer interpret the smile on his boy's face.

"Happy birthday, Mr. Keyes," said Matthew, and turning, walked down the platform and out the station door.

In A Warm Room

Coming home I felt weary and trodden on, as though I was taking up space on the seat of the train, and not simply coming home. I tried to recapture the everyday feeling of going home from work on the tube; but instead, I closed my eyes and thought how I would like to be alone for the evening and not helping entertain Sally's guests. Then, when I opened the front door, Duncan was there.

He was talking to Oliver, Sally's boyfriend. Looking up, he raised his hand and I could feel from the door how he went calm, like he always did. I could hardly say hello. But he continued talking to Oliver so I went to the kitchen where Sally was fumbling around with oven gloves and hot plates.

"Where am I going to put these dinner plates?"

"Where did all these people come from?"

"All *your* friends."

"*One* of them is – watch the potatoes."

"Monica rang – she's coming over later too, I have to leave something for her."

"When did Duncan arrive?"

When I'd spoken to her I felt better. I went in and put my arms around him then and said hello, at last, while he was still talking to Oliver and had to put down his fork in mock surprise, as though I had bowled him over.

"I'd no idea you were coming," I said inanely, hardly conscious of Oliver, or of how I sat in close to the wall, pinned between the table and Duncan's chair.

"North London's a bitch to find your way round," he replied, with the usual irrelevancy that covered an awkward moment.

Soon the conversation round the table broke into two

streams: up where Sally sat there was animated discussion about London taxis, punctuated with peals of laughter as the anecdotes became more and more outrageous. All the while Duncan and I were sinking into a deep quietness at our end of the table. He told me briefly, carelessly, of some things that had happened since we'd last seen each other, and with his words, a period which had seemed an age concertinaed suddenly into a small object of no worth. The black cherries he was lifting methodically with his fork had more importance. "Nothing" I answered, when he asked what I'd been doing, and the way I said it silenced us both for a while.

After dinner, while the others talked over coffee, we slipped out on the balcony for a cigarette. I found myself fighting back the natural small talk that sprang to mind. I didn't want to say "Like old times" to Duncan. I knew how he saw through the outer skins and how absurd I sounded when I spoke anything but the truth to him. It was not like old times.

"London's a comfort" I said instead, boldly. "Same old city, slate and grime and chimneys." I stopped, self conscious.

"Go on," Duncan said gently.

"Well, when I look out over it like this, spires and wet streets, I think of centuries, and I can't understand how a man gets such a short time – his poor threescore years and ten. What's he supposed to accomplish in that? There isn't enough left, even for me.

Duncan said nothing and we stood in silence until the two glowing ends of the cigarettes hissed out on the wet street below.

"Let's walk somewhere," he said, decisively.

On the tube there were two girls with their mother. One was plump, full of good humour, likeable and contented without realising it. Her sister looked older; she was thin, in jeans, and seemed tired but happy. The mother was young-looking with a tanned comfortable face and she enjoyed teasing her daughters. You could see that. I sat stiffly beside Duncan, strangely drawn by a brief interlude in the life of strangers, trying somehow to neutralise the presence, lanky and relaxed, beside me. Now that we were away from the flat, out in the open with nothing familiar but each other, I was afraid. The girls had been out somewhere with their mother and the younger one had had too much cream and she felt sick and was laughing. The mother told her she'd better not be sick because *she* wasn't going to clean it up. She was laughing too. Then she leaned forward and began telling her daughters in a confidential tone the whole carriage could hear, about a man who kept snakes, geckos, and one whole floor of his house was a reptile room. The plump daughter didn't know what a gecko was and the mother said, you know, a snake-thing with an orange eye. "Just one orange eye?" said the daughter, "like this? in the middle?"

They laughed a lot and I didn't want to get off the train. I felt that they were going home to their house (it would be warm and comfortable, lit with lamps – untidy), I could imagine it so clearly, and I wished I did not have to be the one who left the train with Duncan at my side. I felt a knot of giddy anxiety tighten in my stomach. As the train slowed the thin sister was trying to go asleep on the plump one's shoulder. The plump one was ineffectually shrugging her off, while she tried to decide whether or not she had ever seen a picture of a gecko.

Duncan seemed to slip between the doors before they even opened. He was quick, purposeful now and led me to the river, over one bridge and back across another. We read the moving sign over the National Theatre, a line each, until we'd been through the whole programme and our eyes hurt. At the Embankment, life began to pour out everywhere around us and I felt Duncan tighten his step. We were looking for a pub I had told him of, in a small street around Westminster, but as I turned each less familiar corner, my sense of direction became more and more uncertain.

"You're not relaxed yet, are you?" he said. I replied shortly that if I was relaxed I never would have lost my way. In fact the remark frightened me.

"I've been here countless times before," I protested, trying to shake off the feeling and sound controlled. "The streets have this nasty habit of swapping round when you're not there."

Duncan stopped by a statue of some knight he said looked like his old physics master. I reminded him how he'd always made me laugh with imitations of his French teacher, and we talked a bit about school and people neither of us had thought of for a long time. I was quite bright and chatty but he suddenly laid hold of my arm and said -

"You don't really know what to say, do you?"

I was about to protest – so tempting to protest and pass the moment off – but instead, I said,

"No. It's funny, I don't," and we walked on. But while my step was deadened and it appeared suddenly useless to be walking beside him like this, Duncan walked as though reassured of something, and made more confident to proceed in that reassurance. I silently relinquished my role of guide, as he began to work out logically where the pub must be situated and led me down a small street at the end of which we turned right and saw it there, smugly lit up in the wet dusk. As we were going in I thought fleetingly of the mother and her daughters reaching home. They would enter, laughing, one of the warm rooms of an upper storey and throw their coats across the chair backs, complaining of the damp evening they had just closed out.

I found an empty corner while Duncan got the drinks, and sat reflecting on a thought that had been taking shape for a long time. It was an observation about myself which Duncan's arrival had suddenly made tangible. I vacillate, I thought, between having too good and too bad an opinion of myself, There is no middle way. What a revelation! Then I must learn only to think less extremely and I will be content. Duncan set the two glasses down and licked his fingers. The light came nicely through the beer, but I was preoccupied with what to say. We had come to rest, it seemed, after all that motion and again, most acutely, I had nothing to say.

"Now," his tone was final, "tell me something I'll be surprised to hear."

For a moment, I was caught by familiar exasperation: why couldn't he let me talk like other people? like myself? Why these riddles and tests? Then a glimpse of the old freedom, the heady chance to say the kind of thing I never said. All the same, I felt forced into an old mould. I took a deep breath:

"I'm sorry you came now. I wish you hadn't."

"Yeah" he said, and I could not tell if he was surprised.

"Inscrutable as ever."

"You're the inscrutable one!" he accused me playfully. But we were heading for the bone. "You never say what's going on."

"But Duncan – it's *hard*! You make it hard. Coming so suddenly after so long and looking for...I dunno. Who are you looking for?" I felt sheepish, unreal. This was the kind of conversation I was accustomed to overhearing, laughing at and repeating for friends. I felt mean and small suddenly. "I mean, you know – if you're coming to sweep me away to exotic faraway places, I'll chuck the reticence and open my heart but, come on, where's the point?"

"You're bitter." Now he really was surprised.

"I suppose. Yeah, I'm bitter."

"Hm. So I shouldn't have come to see you."

"I don't know." Don't lose courage now! I told myself. "I don't mean to push you away."

It was becoming difficult for me to go on sitting here in this pub, beside this man. An old tension was pulling familiar strings. Something had to come to a head. I wished most of all for a reason to go back out into the damp night streets and hear a little wind in the leaves and place a hand on cold stone by the river.

Duncan drank in silence for a while. Then he felt for his cigarettes and lit one. He passed it to me and lit another. Such a simple gesture; it was hardly calculated to stir up the confusion of sadness and delight that shook my unbalanced heart.

"Thank you," I said. The tension drained out of me. We were friends sharing the old cigarette rite. That was that. There was another long pause and Duncan finished his beer.

"What would you like to do now?"

"Finish my drink. Go home." I smiled, hoping I looked inscrutable.

"Do I get to see you there?" His voice was husky and for a moment I thought, how terrible; he is really hurt; I've done something serious. Then he made a familiar, extravagant gesture of enquiry, drawing himself back and looking foolishly quizzical. He arched his eyebrows till they almost disappeared and then broke into laughter.

'You're a secretive bitch, you know that?"

"Yep. That's me."

"Do you know what you want at all?"

"No."

I smiled, feeling unaccountably serene. A balance had been reached, a middle way. "That's the great thing. I haven't a clue."

We went home by tube. The city had moved into night – the carriage was full of bums, ragged-eyed businessmen, a couple of punks. It was too late for any mothers to be bringing young daughters home. They were, I thought, safely tucked up in bed. Duncan's hand stole easily into mine. They were sleeping now, in a warm room, dreaming of geckos.

Knife

I am the English girl, the graduate student. I sit at dinner with his eyes resting briefly on me from time to time; there is much laughter and the boys are trying their luck. They tease their mother until she warns them to stop. They giggle and spill their lemonade and pinch each other until she sends them from the room.

Later I will be the nurse in the hospital. I will prepare him for surgery and give him something to help him sleep, yes, I will be the night-nurse too. All the women, from every side, touching him with our hands and eyes, or with our voices, a light touch on the arm, the touch of a laugh including him or hands working, deftly washing him in a hospital bed, or the briefest butterfly touch of our eyes. The woman in the store where he pays for the pyjamas. "The receipt is in the bag, sir," smiling at him, holding out the plastic bag.

I have come to dinner. It is the first time we have met. Joclyn called me Saturday lunchtime to invite me.

"An old friend of mine is down. He needs some cheering up."

Joclyn and I laugh a lot when we get together. We keep things for each other, holding anecdotes and caricatures in a part of the brain and then we have dinner and they all surface and the afternoon staggers about, drunk with laughter. The boys join in as well, holding their sides, their round cheeks getting rounder and their blue eyes filling. Sometimes they are the funniest things of all. Max, their father, keeps his laughter low and thoughtful.

I have been studying all morning and my head is full. The sun comes through Joclyn's french doors. He wakes in the dark. "Eat drink and be merry," Joclyn says, raising her glass to him with a smile. She has told me David will be in surgery on Wednesday, but I already know why he starts from sleep at 4am and lies sweating in a waking dream. The knife glints wickedly in the moonlight. Joclyn cooks an excellent nut roast, a real mouthwaterer. The boys are fighting over spoons. Nathan needs a big one. He's a bigger boy. Aaron always has to take the little spoon, it's not fair, mummy it's not fair, Nathan always gets a bigger spoon. Joclyn asks me what I'm working on just now and David's eyes rest briefly on my face. I will be the one who administers. First I will take his name at the desk, I forgot that. I will register him, give him the form to fill out, watch him ink in his name, occupation, date of arrival. Then it is time to be the first nurse: I will take him to the room, draw the curtains round the bed, offer to bring a cup of tea.

Pound, I tell Joclyn. The early poems. The imitations. "The Return," says David softly. *"These were the swift to harry; these the keen scented; these were the souls of blood..."* I am surprised. I did not think him a man with poetry in him, and I notice how it seems he has to clamber over a great wall of shyness to say such a thing. But we begin to talk about Pound and slowly his shyness seems to slip and he becomes animated. He is especially interested in my work. What will my thesis undertake? Who am I interested in? What have I found? His mind is agile and I am glad. It warms me to think that inside the body I will wash and dry, the limbs I will coach back to health after the knife, there is a supple brain. He is sharp, and it will whet his fear. *"You of the finer sense,"* I quote to him under my breath. *"Helpless against the control."*

After dinner, we sit out in the garden and Max plays football with the boys while we have coffee. Joclyn has old deck chairs with wooden arms, the kind you recline in, the kind that swing shut on your fingers when you are folding them away. She is speaking to David about people they know, drawing him somewhere he is reluctant to go. He is withdrawing, slowly and in increasing pain, attempting to retreat to a place where he can be alone with his fear. Joclyn's anecdotes of Louise and Michael and Ben fall short and after an interval of silence during which he stares into space, she bring him back to us with a start – she touches his arm, and instantly I feel a peculiar flurry of jealousy. I will touch him from all sides: I will rearrange the covers as he tosses restlessly at night, I will wheel him to the theatre.

The boys are tired of football; they want some drinks, they want tea, sandwiches, biscuits. Joclyn is laughing but firm. We've only just had dinner.

"Aw mu-um! Can we have ice-creams then?"

"Yeah! Ice-creams!" Aaron, content to support his older brother's ideas, chimes in. Max has flopped, exhausted, in a chair, his head thrown back and his legs wide apart. He's squinting into the sun.

"I'll get them ice-creams," David says quietly. The boys fidget a little, unsure of whether to press the point with this slightly unfamiliar man. They look from their mother to David and back. Joclyn herself seems undecided.

"It'll stretch my legs," David says, deciding the matter.

Watching the three of them leave the garden, the boys close together, a little wary, David walking moodily with his hands in his pockets, I feel compelled to follow them. I want to be with him, I want it to begin now; what if he should walk in front of a truck on the main road, on the way to get ice-creams? What if I should be cheated by a quirk of fate? Closing my eyes, I hold the knife up to the light, this way, now this; the steel is taut, wicked in sunlight as moonlight. I put it away and open my eyes. Joclyn is regarding me with amusement.

"What do you think of him?"

I like her directness. She would like us to get together, I know that, and I envy the simplicity of her scheme. It could be like that: Joclyn, my friend and something of an aunt-figure, older sister perhaps, brings the two of us together on a sunny Sunday. David needs someone now, a friend. What he really needs, Joclyn thinks, is a lover. And that is what I need too, she has been telling me that for ages.

"He's nice." It pleases her, my apparent compliance with her plan. But she's not fooled.

"How nice?"

Max is alert now. He's a decent man, Max, but sometimes his wife's subtleties seem to pass him by.

"Leave her alone Joclyn," he turns his serious eyes to me. "She'd have you two married by Tuesday."

"Oh no," she laughs, but a little mournfully. "Tuesday would not be a good day for poor David."

"No." I am on the verge of weaving a small web, one of the many harmless packets of lies I have fabricated in this matter. What is wrong with him, I am about to ask. What's the op for? After all, it would seem only natural to be curious about it, and to broach the subject with him temporarily out of earshot. But the words stick in my throat. I can't put on the innocent little act. For an awful moment it is not innocent; it is foul, dangerous; it is obscene. Obscurely ashamed, I turn from my friends and look down their long garden. The grass is uneven, a little too long. The path is cracked. It's a green, comfortable garden.

Joclyn and Max are discussing David now, Joclyn with interest, Max indifferently. I get up, unwilling to be drawn into the discussion, dissatisfied suddenly, restless. Their kitchen is cool and I pour myself a glass of water. The ice clinks distantly and I stand at the sink, looking out at my friends sitting chatting on their lawn. The pictures that were so clear in my head at dinner have faded. Their colours are washed out. When David left with the boys, he seemed to take the edge off the situation. The urgency went with him. Soon they will be back, the boys clamouring and sticky, hungry for attention. I could stay on, have tea with them; maybe David would offer to see me home. Time alone with him...a decision is reached abruptly and I leave the water half drunk on the draining board.

"Joclyn?" I'm hanging out of the back door, one arm holding the towel rail, calling out in a voice I hope is nonchalant. It is suddenly an urgent matter that I leave before he gets back. I must sit alone all evening. I must think long and carefully about what will be done. "I'm going to head now, I think."

Joclyn reaches round in her deckchair. "You won't stay for tea?" She's disappointed in me, thwarting her little arrangement like this. She didn't really think I would fall in obediently with the plan, but she hoped at least we'd all have tea together, maybe in the garden. Joclyn likes to be surrounded by people, people she has gathered to her; two over-active kids are not enough for her.

"Nope. I want to get back to Ezra. Got to keep the momentum up."

"David will never marry you if you run away like this." Max is teasing his wife now, smiling broadly. She waves an arm at him dismissively.

"Never mind. Never mind, next time you can give Ezra the slip for a whole day. It'll be better for David too."

I leave them, slipping round the side of the house where David walked just minutes before. There is no one on the street. I turn away from the main road and check once before I turn the corner that the three of them had not come into view and seen me walking, almost hurrying in the opposite direction.

Sunday evening at home, then, in the high-ceilinged rooms I share with the late summer light and my cat. The floors are cool. It is six o'clock. It is necessary now, essential, to sit in the stillness, on the window seat, the cushions arranged in their special way, the window open wide so the street sounds will call me back in the end; to sit like that and think through as much of what will happen as I can. Earlier, I was uncomfortable with the thing; the lapse of colours worried me. Now I have time.

It seems the matter will begin at the registration desk of the Douglas Regent Memorial Hospital. The woman in the pyjama store is a distraction. I do not need the sight through her eyes, the brush of David's hand as he takes the plastic bag. No, I am firm now, the matter will begin in the hospital. From the moment he signs his name, he will be in my hands. For an hour, perhaps, while the light loses focus in the street, I am lost in the corridors;

I am dressed in white, brisk and efficient. I administer. I prepare.

September first is a blank day in his diary. He does not have anything inked in: no appointments, no films he wants to see. His eye has caught it every time and the pupil winced. What could he write? "The Big One"? "Hospital 2.30"? But when he is at last sitting on the bed with the curtains drawn, filtering out the heartless sunlight, no amount of preparation can have made him ready and I, as the first nurse, have to prompt him: "Would you like to undress now", before he can emerge from the frozen, rabbit-like panic and realise that this is what he must do. I'll come back in five minutes to make him comfortable, I say. In five minutes he is sitting stiffly in the bed, his clothes folded neatly on the end. For a moment, I falter at the curtain: even as nurse, efficient, flinty, I feel a flicker of panic myself.

What now?

I return with a jolt to the window seat and the cooling street. Across the rooftops of the abandoned theatre and the school beyond, I can just see the hospital. In this light it is a mellow red, but I know to David it will look forbidding as a jail. Then the idea occurs, unfolding slowly, and I swing my legs off the windowseat and begin to pace the room. The cat pads in and stands, unmoved, in the doorway. When I have passed her twice she pads with dignity to the window, hesitates, then jumps neatly onto the cushions I have warmed. As she curls up, her tail twitches twice, imperiously.

"Pandora," I tell her, "you lazy dumb cat. *Tomorrow* is the day of rest. Tomorrow you lie in a ball and collect your wits. Today we are still thinking."

Apart from the flick of her ear when she hears her name, she ignores me completely.

All day Monday I work with a rare concentration. In the morning, I comb my notes for references and type a bibliography with meticulous care: it is a job I hate, but this morning I do it with a kind of jubilance. All afternoon, I lie on the board floor, writing furiously. The work is taking shape. The thesis idea so long hedged around, weighed up inconclusively and politely despised, blossoms easily. The air in the room hums with summer, and I swing my legs, exulting in the ease with which things are accomplished. At six o'clock, precisely twenty-four hours after I returned from Joclyn's, I drop down to Lucky's and fill a basket with lunchtime treats. Sauntering along the aisles full of people stale from their Monday's work, I purse my lips and try to concentrate on what David might like to eat for lunch. Avocadoes stuffed with prawns? Blue cheese dip with crackers? Blueberry muffins and some Java special brew? In the end, I decide on the lot, and round it up with a bottle of Spanish wine and a quart of gin.

Tuesday is a clear, still day. I wake cleanly and lie with my eyes closed, experimentally dressing myself in white. Nurses uniforms are starched. White tights – ugh! – and – ugh! ugh! – sensible shoes. Smiling to myself, I shower and pull on my simplest, shortest cotton dress. It makes me look about twelve years old, and after making twelve-year-old faces in the mirror for a while, I take it off and choose instead a short grey skirt and loose shirt. Then there is the choice of bag: the black leather duffel or the tapestry shoulder bag? Which of the two should I be swinging as I make my way down Solomon Street, right past the terrace of Mo's? It is only ten thirty. There is ample time for these trivial considerations. Though in the light of what is to come, they are hardly trivial. They are definitely not trivial. When I have chosen bag and shoes and stuffed some of my books and a jotter in the duffel, I set the answering phone. It occurs to me I should perhaps ring Joclyn. Is it part of the day? What would I say to her? How would it fit? How would it constitute a missing piece?

It is not part of the day; relieved it didn't have to be, I pull the front door to and set off down the stairs. I haven't eaten, so my head feels deliciously light when I take the first drag of a cigarette. Naughty naughty, nurse, I tell myself in my crispest tones. Smokers die younger.

Whether because of the cigarette or not, my heart is

beating uncomfortably by the time I reach the end of the road. There is the corner of Solomon Street, the butcher's window, gaping with sinews, bald bone, horrible fatted sides of meat. In the back of the shop the butcher's knife will be quick. They are brothers, surgeon and butcher. Unexpectedly, my gorge rises and I stop by the wall, a hand out to touch the solidity of brick and mortar. I stand there a moment, shocked by the reality of what I am doing: take a walk down Solomon Street, I whisper to myself, and you never know who you might meet. It sounds exactly like a child's nursery rhyme, with the same menacing undercurrents, the backdrop of threat I remember vividly: if you go down to the woods today...you must never go down to the end of the town...But I do know who I would meet. He is there already. As I turn the corner, I know he is there, alone on the terrace with a pot of tea, his hands circling the cup, his gaze faraway and troubled.

By the bookshop, if I look across, I will see him. The crossing is right by Mo's. This side is the small boutique with the leggings in the window I thought of buying all last week. The lights are green and I keep my eyes on the traffic as I wait to cross, hand on the white rope of the duffel bag. Red orange yellow green, these are the colours I have seen. I need a child's rhyme now, some words to chant as I cross the road and come so close – instead the words that come are Eliot's and I mutter them, my lips moving. *The wounded surgeon plies the steel that questions the distempered part, beneath the bleeding hands we feel the sharp –*

"Hello!"

"David!" I stop a foot from the terrace balustrade, and he half stands, scraping his wooden chair, then sits again awkwardly. He is taking me in, those same eyes that became animated when he quoted poetry.

"How's Pound?"

"Oh -" I pat the bag and laugh gaily, "he's a heavy weight."

He barely smiles. The anxiety is plain to me, but I'm in automatic now, balancing on a wave that should wash me smoothly round to sit across from him over tea and a friendly conversation. It happens like that. He asks where I am going, how come I'm in the neighbourhood.

"But I live just over there!" I point and a butterfly of pride folds her wings in a pretty gesture over my heart. What a plan. What a perfect, seamless plan. I accept his invitation with just the correct degree of hesitation and,as I pass behind him into the gloom of Mo's to order fresh tea, allow myself a single indulgence of imagination: David on his back, under the lights, in victim's green, slipping from consciousness. Don't worry David, I know my stuff and the knife is keen. You won't feel a thing.

When I bring the tea he is sitting in the same position, hugging his elbows, watching the street, seeing his own grim fantasies in the traffic and the passersby. It will be easy from here, horribly easy. I set the teapot down and slip onto the chair opposite. Nothing can stand in my way.

"So how come you're having tea in my favourite cafe? You don't live nearby as well, do you?"

"No." He stirs his tea, deliberating. "I have to go over there later." He gestures back towards the hospital.

"Oh my gosh yes! Of course, today's the day!" I take a drink. The tea is bitter black. "Poor old you." I leave another moment. "Nervous?"

"Well," he purses his lips, undecided: am I an unwelcome distraction in these final hours or should he give himself over to the opportunity to divert his mind? A flicker of unease seems to pass over him. "Yes, I am. I'm pretty scared, actually." He searches my face, looking for something – reassurance? A sign of comfort? And mine will be the capable hands. I embody the system he will be trundled smoothly through. It would be nice, I reflect briefly, to let him know it will all be ok. I would like to tell him what would lift this worry from his shoulders now. But that's absurd.

"Oh dear. What time do you check in?"

"Two thirty. Surgery...tomorrow morning."

"Two thirty. Hmm." Better cover some neutral ground

first. "I'm sorry I disappeared on Sunday without saying goodbye."

"Oh that's alright. Those kids can be a little much."

"No it wasn't that. I can cope with the kids. I wanted to do some work. I had an idea that afternoon."

He nods, but there isn't the spark of interest there was on Sunday afternoon. It's probably hard for him to feel interested in anything, I reason. There is a boulder in the forefront of his mind, the weight of this experience he must get beyond, and he cannot think very clearly of anything else. Nevertheless, I begin a brief synopsis of the pages I wrote yesterday, the direction my arguments are leading me, the hopes I have for an early completion. He half-listens. He looks tired. The skin below his eyes is a bad mushroom colour. "You didn't sleep last night, did you?"

He draws back a little and seems to shrink away as though I have accused him of something. Come on man, I think, momentarily scornful, is there a backbone in there? He mumbles something then and I try to summon the enthusiasm to set the next phase in motion. It is all working out so exactly as planned that I am beginning to feel maybe this, after all, is not worth the time and effort I am investing. The time alone – twenty four hours a day for goodness knows how long, until he is out of hospital and back in real life, and this when I am just cracking the nut of my thesis. And then there is the effort: the concentration, the mental precision. All those long hours of deep, dangerous meditation – the foundation laying, the whole process of preparation leading up to Joclyn's long-awaited invitation to Sunday lunch.

Joclyn, I think, watching a small child trying to drag its father back to the toyshop window on the other side of the road. Joclyn, you mean so well. I value your friendship, that's the truth. I don't know what I am to you – a surrogate younger sister, maybe, the bright, somewhat aloof English girl you like to go to the theatre and out for Thai food with. My thoughts wander for a little around her house, Max and the kids; I see again the garden as it looked on Sunday afternoon, long and green and untroubled. I almost forget where I am, sitting outside Mo's with David, about to take another of the important steps that will lead us to the knife.

"How about coming back to my place for some lunch?"

It is time to be direct. No point beating around this bush since the outcome is already clear. While he is making some feeble objections about my work, and taking up my time, I'm wondering whether we should eat cross-legged on the sitting room floor or at the white wooden kitchen table. Of course we pay the bill and leave Mo's together. Of course he almost forgets to bring with him the Weingreen's bag with his new pyjamas, toothbrush and razor blades.

"That's all you've got?" I ask, amused. "For a stay in hospital?"

He looks embarrassed.

"I couldn't think what else I might need."

I allow myself a hearty laugh.

"David! You're such a typical -" I sober quickly, seeing he looks hurt, lost almost. "Dear me. You know what? I'll have to pop in to see you and bring something to keep you from dying of boredom. Would you mind?" I add seriously, turning to him as we pass the boutique. He is about to answer when I swing back hurriedly to the window. It is not that I have remembered the brightly coloured leggings; it is not a fear of what he is about to answer – but a sudden contraction of my own fear.

What? I am walking up Solomon Street with David Layton, a man I met for the first time two days ago. It is eleven thirty. It is August 31st. Before September is a day old I will know what it is like to cut this man open. But I am an English PhD student – I am a student nurse, a secretary, an anaesthetist – I am twenty four – I am losing ground – I don't know -

A claw of panic tightens round my insides. Stop this now! Stop this horrible thing! I don't want it – it is not natural.

The panic subsides as quickly as it rose; I have only been gone a moment. We are walking down Solomon Street.

"That would be very nice," says David.

I am back on course. Phase two is well underway.

David would like some wine but he isn't hungry.

"Can't I tempt you with stuffed avocadoes? Blueberry muffins?" I call from the kitchen. He is perusing my bookshelves. Pandora sneaks in the kitchen door and rubs dreamily against my leg. "Hello Pan. Have a nice doze then?"

"No thank you," he calls from the other room. The sun is slanting across the kitchen table, deciding me that this is where we should eat lunch. But it's still only twenty to twelve. I mix myself a weak gin sling and bring the wine, opener and a glass into the sitting room. Everything has settled again, and I look forward to the three hours ahead, a quiet interlude before I have to slip into those unbecoming white tights, and the chores of the afternoon.

David is standing by the window, flipping through a copy of The Golden Bough, which I know he is not really looking at.

"A glass of wine, then?" I curl up on the window seat with my own glass and watch him expertly pour himself some ruby red wine. "Cheers!"

There follows an hour of conversation. I put a Neil Young record on and notice that he seems to relax a little. While he tells me about growing up in Washington DC, the only child of a woman widowed at 32, I look at his fingers, his knuckles, the lobes of his ears. It thrills me that soon he will be between crisp sheets and mine will be the hands that touch and smooth, in a way I cannot touch now. It's funny, I think, the little intimacies that a nurse robs of every vestige of sensuality. I must remove my rings, I think absently, turning the silver bands on my right hand. When he pours himself a third glass of wine I am not sure if I should say something. Maybe his tolerance is very high. Maybe he *wants* to fortify his courage with a little more than is strictly prudent. The flush in his cheeks as he raises the glass doesn't reassure me, however. For a moment the edge of the glass sparkles and I am seeing the knife. Don't forget the knife, David.

He's asking how I came out here and I answer briefly. My concentration is slipping, as though the wine were affecting me too. He's getting through the third glass at quite a rate.

"I think I'll have a glass myself," I say brightly, going to the kitchen to rinse my tumbler. It is 12.36. The apex of the day is past and the sun already seems lower, warming the downward slopes of the day.

Don't mess things up now, David, I murmur, and the shadow of a doubt flutters darkly by.

By 1.30 he is drunk. There is no question. He politely declines all offers of stuffed avocadoes and blue cheese dip, but thinks he might have a gin sling.

"That's what you were drinking, wasn't it?" he says, enunciating with care.

"Yes." I head furiously for the kitchen. There is nothing to be done but let him drink himself silly and hope he doesn't lose his way from my door to the DRM. You fool, you bloody fool, I tell myself, mixing the drink. The bathroom door bangs and I close my eyes. He probably hasn't eaten for twenty four hours, and now four glasses of wine in two. When he reappears, I am sitting frostily in a straight-backed chair, flipping quickly through a magazine.

"I'm sorry to be taking up your time," he says. "You must have plenty of work to do. I think perhaps -" he puts a hand out to the doorframe. I stand.

"Are you alright?"

"I think perhaps I'll have one drink and be on my way." He smiles. There is something unexpected in the smile, something unwelcome. It is satisfaction. From the moment he leaves the doorway, I believe I have lost. I believe it is all a game I have been playing – with Joclyn and Max, Pound, Pandora and Mo's Cafe. It has all been an extravagant joke.

"David?"

But he doesn't answer at once. He is draining his gin sling, downing it in one, and through the distortions of the glass it looks as though he's still smiling.

"David -" I touch his arm. The first touch is *not* the nurse's cool hand, then; it is my urgent one. But there's no point. He turns to me a grin as handsome, as genuine as sin.

"I'm leaving now, thank you. Thank you very much, you've been a wonderful time. Tell me, is there a station near here? A bus station?"

Primary Colours

A house on a river. I could winter there like an animal going underground. Willows sleeping heavily over the water. There are always willows and the kitchen is stone and seems to root in the earth. Living there would come as naturally as breathing. Sartre writes about a man who exercised his right to life without a doubt. I read every night until the insides of my eyes are red. It is difficult to stay up all night reading Sartre when you have to be at work the next day. At work they tell me there is something wrong with me, that I am falling asleep all the time. I tell them it runs in my family. We all have our eyes set very deep and we all sleep a lot. My younger son is like this too. He plants himself in the bed and grows there all night. The older one sleeps like a leaf, he is like his father. There he stands at four in the morning, framed in my doorway, mumbling. The door is creaking, he says. There's a tapping going on at the window. His bed moves. Poor Aaron, he can hear a bat flip his wing and it is a scratch on his soul, an irritant. Now he stands in the door and I know it has not reached the time my brain is responsible for waking up.

"The lightshade is wearing wellingtons," he mumbles. I wake him. "Aaron, try to go back to bed," but he says a brown man is at the front door. I have learned to trust such instincts. The man at the front door is leaning on the bell which doesn't work and when I open the door on the chain he topples inwards. It is Louis Waterson, my husband's old friend. When I let him in he lies down on the hall floor. "It's comfortable," he says, "just leave me here." But Louis is a good friend of David's, I liked him from the start, and he is caked in mud. If he lies there all night I will have to shampoo the carpet.

"Get up," I tell him. "Have some gin." I remember he likes gin, drinks it from milk bottles. It's a smelly drink but I think David keeps a bottle in the bathroom cabinet. Louis tries to get up, but his legs seem heavier than usual and he would prefer to stay where he is. I explain about the carpet and that the kitchen is warmer and we get there with me holding him under the arms. I don't know if you have ever held anyone under the arms, it is a very private thing. Aaron watches with his eyes rounder than usual. "Go to bed kid," says Louis as he is helped down the hall. "Go and hang out with your teddy bear." He says it kindly, though.

I fetch the gin and pour some in a tumbler. "None for you!" Louis says in surprise. He can't believe I don't want to drink gin at five in the morning in my nightshirt. "Got any beer? You have some beer." He insists I have a beer. David and him, both of them, they could never drink alone. You had to do it too, in all situations, any time of the day or night. Driving me to the hospital with Michael coming, my stomach tight as a drum and no shoes on, David whipped out a quart at the lights. "Have some," he insisted, "I need it."

"You look skinnier," Louis says. The gin is firing through his blood and he is looking round him. "Last time you were big as a house. That the kid out there?"

"Gosh, no, that's the older one. Michael's only three. He doesn't wake."

"Did I make a noise? I hit the bell a bit. It was a mistake. I forgot to get off it."

He sees me looking at the mud all down his jacket, caked on his face. His eyes blear out from it, pale and humorous. "Oh yeah – the mud. I tried something that didn't work." That's all I'm going to get by way of explanation. It's ok, I just want to get back to bed. Sleep is pounding inside my skull, trying to be let out, but the beer and Louis's conversation work together and I can feel my limbs getting all the nervous energy of a headless chicken running round the chicken yard. We're talking about railways, always a big subject with Louis, and about David. He's in Chicago now, I tell him, and that brings us to the city where we all grew up. There is a certain time of the morning when speaking with a person who grew up where you did is like sharing a bowl of water in the desert. You feed off each other greedily and you fight about the names of streets in the place.

"That's not where Scoobys' Toys and Collectibles was for chrissake. We're way south of Division Street here -"

"I *lived* opposite the place till I was seven!..."

You bandy the city about between you, dissect it like an old familiar intriguing puzzle, and then you lovingly put it back together again and you are soulmates.

At about 6.30 we check the kids, Louis takes a shower, and we go for breakfast in Stanley's: plates of bacon and more beer. Louis hasn't finished with Chicago but I am eager to find out what he's been doing for three years. "I can't go into all that now," he says. "Too much." He is silent for a bit. I tell him I dream of living on a river with willows. "Bare in the winter," he says. "All those long skinny branches. Best in the spring. Little green down of leaves." I don't feel I am exercising my right to life without a doubt, I tell him. I can mention this now we have covered Chicago and the talk of being kids there. "You're right," says Louis. He tells me a story about travelling on the lorries bringing fruit up over the Himalayas. The lorries travel in convoys and sometimes they cross the mountains when the roads are not yet fully passable. Once he changed lorries at a stopover. He liked to ride on the last lorry so he could look down the mountains to the end of the world and think he was the only one there, but this day he changed lorries and on a high ridge the last lorry skidded and went over the edge. "I didn't feel lucky," Louis says. "I said 'that's my right' and I was angry because it was his right too, the guy who drove the truck. He had a wife and three kids waiting for him to get back."

It's time for the kids to wake up for school. "Already?" Louis stretches painfully. Aaron will be rummaging in the laundry basket for his favourite shorts. Every day is the same, he wants to wear the blue shorts he wore the day after the last wash. I explain about the shorts and washing and how you can only wear your favourite shorts once a week. He still wants to wear them. Michael will be burrowing up from sleep, unfurling, looking for light. I have got to be there for them when they wake up, wearing my green fluffy dressing gown. It's very important for them, these primal things. The red milk jug we have always had – Michael checks for it every morning. He feasts his eye on it for a tiny moment, I see him do it and then he is able to begin his day. I am stiff too from drinking beer and talking in the kitchen since five. Why do we do these things? I can't do them any more without feeling ninety years old by mid-morning. I have the feeling I've lost something, and I tell Louis about this too. "Your tail," he says. "We have never felt right since we lost our tails." I pay the bill and when I get back he is asleep at the table. Stanley takes my spare key and says he'll give it to him when he wakes. He looks too peaceful to disturb.

Yes. We are helpless because we no longer have a tail. Maybe Scoobys' Toys and Collectibles wasn't on Division street after all. I can't think about it any more, my sons are waking up, I've got to get the red milk jug on the kitchen table. Crossing Main Street I step out when I feel the lights will change, and the cars pulse in harness, growling. There isn't much hope for later in the morning, but now I suddenly feel well. Maybe Louis will stay a few days when he wakes up and take the kids to a railway show. Or maybe he'll be gone and the key will be at Stanley's when I get home. He is right about the willows – they're not a winter tree. It has to be Spring. Maybe in the Spring, me and the boys, a quiet river, the smell of bread baking in a stone kitchen. I'm laughing at myself, with my key in the door. There's the kids to get ready for school, the signs of gin and a beer bottle to clear away, a casserole to get ready for dinner, and I'm walking in the dark looking in at lighted windows.

Aaron gives a thin cry in the bedroom. The shorts

conversation will begin in a moment. Standing in the hall I have a moment of the clearest wellbeing. It starts at the back of my shoulders and creams down my back. "Get on with it, you half-baked fool," I tell myself, "get to the business," and I'm laughing to myself.

Saxifrage

The woman was talking about kids on drug programmes and Marcia blinked several times as though clearing her vision would help her remember her name. She looked away briefly. Maybe looking freshly at the woman would bring the name back. Across the room Frank was in an attitude of leaving. He stood uncertainly talking to Sam Moreau's wife and he was trying to wrap up the conversation. He put his empty glass on the bookshelf behind him and nodded quickly several times. Marcia realised with a constriction around her heart that he was going to come over to her and they would leave then. They were going away from this room where people stood at the french doors eating pineapple and cheese on cocktail sticks and sat on the couches with their shoes kicked off talking animatedly about houseplants and shares.

She hadn't wanted to come. A lot of people gathering at the Harris's on a Sunday afternoon, talking about the same old things. She had left it until the last moment to dress. While Frank put on a shirt and tie she sat in the old red armchair looking at a magazine, her legs tucked under her. She wasn't even wearing stockings. Then Frank was in the hall, fixing his tie at the mirror, and she flicked the pages faster, seeing only a blur of car advertisements – he was in the doorway looking down at her and she knew his expression without meeting his eye.

"Shall we hit the road then?" Frank passed his hand down her back now, and smiled at the woman. "Hi Bonnie."

"Oh," Marcia felt a sudden need to hear Bonnie talk on about the kids on the drug programmes. "Frank-"

she felt a little short of breath, "Bonnie was just telling me something very interesting, weren't you Bonnie?" She turned back to the woman and smiled uncertainly. It was a pleasure to say the name and she wanted the opportunity to use it a few more times, to talk on about the kids and other things, to ask Bonnie what she did, where she worked, if she had kids herself.

"We'd better go," Frank said decisively. Marcia felt defeated. They had to leave. Some couples had already gone, there was a knot of people in the hall promising they would call one another. Bonnie was ready to turn to someone else.

"Don't you think," Marcia burst out as though with the last of her breath, "it's odd to be leaving a party just after six? Afternoon parties are so...strange!" She *was* feeling strange. Twenty past six, they were leaving a party. Sunday. What was she normally doing at twenty past six on a Sunday? Frank held her arm and was leading her to the door. She took a last look over her shoulder. Bonnie had her bag open and was rummaging as though for a lipstick. "Bye Bonnie!" she called brightly. Bonnie looked up briefly but didn't seem to see her.

Frank steered her firmly down the hall. She knew several of the people vaguely but there was no time to do more than call goodbye. Lynn Harris was standing at the top of the stairs with two men. Frank called to her that it had been a lovely afternoon and she waved a cigarette lighter at them. Call us back, Marcia thought. Tell us we mustn't go yet. But Lynn was telling a funny story to her guests. Marcia looked at the flowers bordering their front path. The lawn was freshly mowed and the smell of damp cut grass brought a pang to her heart. Her father, cutting the lawn on a Saturday, his hair flopping down in his eyes and his unlit pipe clenched grimly between his teeth. What were those small pink flowers? You could chew the stems, they had a bitter flavour. She used to do it as a kid. Not alyssum, that was white. These were little pink, fragile things.

"Marcia," Frank said. She was standing on the other side of the car from him, staring across the roof. "I've

74

opened it." The car was blue. Was it theirs? Surely their car wasn't blue. She bent down and peered in at the back window. That was how you knew your own car when you came out of the shopping centre or the airport: the old road maps, wrappers, gloves. There was a Mars wrapper and a yellowed newspaper. Could be anyone's car. But Frank was starting up and he leaned over and tapped on her window. "It's open!" she heard him repeat, through the glass. His voice was faraway. If she stayed out here, on the curb, would he drive away without her? Sitting into the passenger seat she saw herself going back up the path and into the clogged hall. She could find Bonnie and ask about the drug programme. She could ask her if she knew what the pink flowers were called.

They turned out onto the main road from the Harris's quiet street. "Bob's been playing golf all week," Frank said. "Says his swing's got ten times better. He's looking great actually." He checked his mirror and changed lanes. "He's in deep mourning for Greta Garbo. Got six of her films out on video on Tuesday." Greta Garbo, Marcia thought, Marilyn Monroe, Brigitte Bardot. Seems like it helped to have your name end in 'o' if you wanted to be a film star. Frank was heading for the freeway exit and she realised uneasily they'd soon be on the bridge. The sky was gathering a sort of deep grey. It looked huge, a tremendous expanse across the bay, with the moving pinpricks of planes. More cars coming back down to the valley than heading East across the bridge. Couldn't they go back? You didn't turn on the freeway, it had to be now, on the main road. Couldn't they turn and go the way everyone else was going? Back to the party. Mombresia, was that the name? No, they'd been in the garden too, along the wall, tightly closed. Mombresia were orange and flowered in July. She smoothed her skirt down and watched the cars as they reached the entrance to the freeway. So fast! And all going somewhere. They all knew where they were going.

"You look lovely in that," Frank said suddenly. She was surprised and glanced at him.

"This?" she said anxiously. He'd had a haircut that Friday and the cropped hairs at the base of his neck seemed to bristle. She was afraid of the look, it was a severe haircut, ugly. His hand on the gearstick seemed perilously close to her leg, almost touching but not quite. They might touch any moment if the car went over a bump. San Mateo Bridge 3. The sign went over their heads. Three miles left and then the long arm out into the bay, skinny and crooked like an old man's.

"Rita's going to quit her job," Frank said. "She reckons she'll never move up in there. She's got ambition."

Marcia closed her eyes. They were burning, as though she'd been crying. Staring into the dusk did it. Never read when the light's going, her father always said, you don't realise how dark it is, the change is gradual. She opened them again and it seemed a lot darker. The last light was behind them, wasn't it? So they were heading into the dark, plunging right into night. All those cars were following the last of the light. Why were they running from it?

The car climbed the ramp onto the bridge and the steel girders loomed over them. Grey bars on both sides. And below – the water! Frank had begun to hum. They were streaming in a flow of cars along a narrow road needling out precariously into the Bay. It was so fragile. Couldn't they stay on land? She felt her stomach contract. It was dreadful, this intrusion out over the water. It was a thing of man. Nature meant people to stay on the land. Small boats rocking, tiny specks in the mass of water, capsized. Huge ocean liners were crushed by icebergs and went down, sucking the air into a huge trough after them, disappearing, without a trace.

"Frank," she said loudly. It was necessary that they go back at once. They were already in sight of the slope down the causeway part; the knotty old man's elbow, the rheumy joint. It was too late!

"I don't want to go on the bridge," she said, but she seemed to speak in a tiny voice, hardly audible over the rushing in her ears, certainly not over the engine. They were doing 70.

"You don't want to what?" Frank said. He was changing into the fast lane. She shook her head. The little pink flowers – why couldn't she remember their name? It began with S. Not sassafras, not sassafras, that was a tree.

She gripped her hands tightly together and the car took the bend of the bridge smoothly. The causeway! Now they were on the narrow stretch running straight across to the East Bay. Seven miles, she remembered it was that far across to the shore. Surely it couldn't be that far? The lights on the other side were well defined now, winking in the hills and in lines along the roads. People were going home. What were they going home from at seven on a Sunday evening? The game? Too late for church. Little back streets where the dark was swallowing up houses. Bad lighting. It was swallowing up whole roads, blanketing the things that went on there, things that were only done in the secrecy of darkness. If it could just hold off for a bit! Her mind paused on the brink of a dark street in the city and edged down close to a high wall. Graffiti, broken glass. The further in, the darker it would get, and all the secrets that the dark kept, she found herself holding her breath tightly – it was fearful things, murders, stabbings, rape, they were all going on, at that moment, over there in the stretch of bulky land they were racing towards. She shook her head quickly as though to rid her mind of the images but they were gathering there, broken windows, shadowy figures, hands raised in violence. She felt dread grip her. They must turn back! How many miles left? Six? Five?

"Frank," she said again, feeling panic tighten her throat. "Let's go back."

He heard her but she hoped he didn't detect the panic. She mustn't appear irrational. Was it irrational not ever to want to reach the shore? Wasn't the bridge as bad, that narrow sliver of earth?

"Huh? Back?"

"No, no," she retracted hurriedly. To reach the shore would be to get off the bridge. But the darkness! The crimes that would be springing up everywhere, doors beaten down, bottles smashing, children would be screaming; it was children who suffered, and young girls. Frank had said something. She took a deep breath.

"No, not back. How far is it to shore now?"

"Well I dunno. About four miles. Looks pretty, doesn't it?"

Pretty? Even the lights were menacing. Tiny wicked pin-pricks, sharp stars. What were the flowers called? Abruptly she began to cry, convulsive sobs, the tears running unchecked down her cheeks and dripping onto the silk blouse Frank thought she looked lovely in. All the way to the shore she cried, with Frank offering to pull over, to stop the car, asking her over and over what the matter was. What was the matter? She held her temples and kept her eyes tightly shut, the land getting closer and closer. What was the *matter*?

Frank checked his mirror and brought the car to the side of the road where there was a stretch of gravel. They were off the bridge, off the freeway, back on the road to their hometown. It was a deserted district, old warehouses, silent trucks. He reached across and laid a hand on his wife's knee.

"Marcia, what is it? Tell me."

"I can't –" she began tearfully, "I can't remember the name of those little pink flowers. You know the ones –" she gave a sob –"the ones Lynn has by her path. They're pink." She hid her face in her hands and sobbed. "You can eat the stems."

The Sky's Gone Out

Before he opened his paper, he glanced down the row of faces opposite. He was not looking for anything. His mind was on an incident at the office that is lost to him now if he tries to recall. It amused him how the English scrutinised each other in the Underground, planted in their rows like beans. He liked to catch two people watching one another without their eyes ever meeting. Yet when he was caught looking someone full in the face, he quickly averted his eyes. If it was a woman, even a plain woman, he was aware he often blushed. Frequently when the carriage was empty he played the game with himself in the window opposite. On good days he risked a wink or a wry smile. In general, he was troubled by his weight and thinning hair, and looked quickly away.

He liked to see a pretty face on the tube. He liked to know without looking that a slender leg was three feet from his own; the hollow of an ankle could arouse in him a peculiar melancholy that was pleasant. Sooner or later he always became engrossed in his paper. Sometimes he thought of his wife for a little: not in clear pictures, but in words and abstractions. She was a gentle woman.

He had a theory: on days when a lovely woman sat across from him, there would invariably be three or four more in the carriage. On these days he did not notice the twelve stations go by. Even the men seemed exemplary specimens. He would smile to himself, thinking what a flaw in the design he was. The lower buttons on his shirt gaped, his trouser legs rode up. He didn't mind. If, on the other hand, an ugly woman sat opposite, her companions were likely to be drab.

Everyone's hair looked greasy. Dandruff prevailed.

The train was full but not crowded, and he got a seat at once: his favourite, at the end. With pleasure he folded his paper and patted it down in his lap. In his first, cursory glance he saw her, but the tiny sound he made involuntarily in his throat was swallowed easily by the train's hum. Suddenly, he had no desire to scan the rest of the faces opposite, nor to make out the reflections of his neighbours in the windows. He looked quickly at his paper. He had read the first paragraph twice. He felt a strong desire to look at her again. She might be getting off at the next station; like hundreds before her, she would disappear in the crowd. Beauty was made to be gratefully admired. He raised his eyes. She was staring an inch to the left of him. She looked transfixed, the word came to him, clear as a bell. Hurriedly he looked away, annoyed with himself, but at the same time acutely troubled. He felt a sensation at the back of his neck and knew it must be the beginning of a blush. Her look! He stared at a point on the door, struggling to think why her look troubled him so greatly. Certainly she was striking. She had the bone structure of a very lovely woman, her hair was silky and escaped from her black felt hat in the kind of tangled curls he particularly liked. Who did she resemble? No one. He realised he had never seen another woman like her. But it was not her face that kept him in this suddenly heightened state – it was her expression. She had stared a little to one side of him with a look of wildness, there was no other way to describe it.

Stiffly, he returned to his paper and read the same paragraph. His eyes fixed on the last word, unseeingly, as he realised that the train was slowing at a station. Once again, she might get off. She might leave. In ten seconds he could be staring at an empty seat, unable to believe she was no longer there. He had to look at the face one more time. His sense of foolishness was uncomfortable, but as the train stopped and she did not move, he let relief embolden him and glanced across. Her eyes were closed.

He did not hear the babble of alighting and movement

in the train around him. For a moment he held his breath. He felt a brief, unidentifiable ache in his abdomen. She sat very still, almost stiffly, with her hands loose on her lap. Her clothes were dark – he took them in confusedly, tensely aware that at any second she might open her eyes and look at him. An infinitesimal scene tripped through his head: she saw him, she was angry, she shouted something, reached across and slapped his face. He felt a hot blush spreading from the roots of his hair, he could feel the tingling on his cheek that followed the sharp impact of her hand.

On her lap, the fingers of one hand clenched suddenly into a fist, then relaxed. She wore no rings. Her eyes were still closed: he allowed himself three agonisingly long seconds taking in the lashes, the cheekbones, the perfect skin, then looked dazedly back down at the paper in his lap. He brought one hand out from under it and studied his nails with care. Details like the white of his cuticles brought him slowly back to rational thought. My god she's lovely. He thought the words once, loudly, then felt a delicious, tantalizing power. If he read his paper for a little longer, before they reached the next station, he could turn the page and take the natural opportunity to glance idly round the carriage. It bothered him that someone might have seen him staring at her, seen the incriminating blush. He wanted to look around defensively, aggressively even, to subdue any knowing looks he might receive. But I am ridiculous, he thought, and again the words came loud and clear. Ridiculous. An old ass. He thought with a smile of his son's latest phrase: a spa. You're a spa daddy. He had rebuked him for using it just the other day.

The train slowed and all thoughts were wiped from his mind. He turned the page of his paper with difficulty. Despite years of practice the paper refused to fold. It rucked in the middle, the inside pages slipped sideways; it was a mess, and the train had stopped. Still, she did not move and he felt absurdly like laughing. One more, then, one more indulgence. At last he got the paper straight. She was staring down now, directly at his feet. He felt his toes stiffen. Briefly he tried to picture his shoes: which ones was he wearing? What colour socks? Her hands were moving in her lap now, a vague fumbling movement – but her eyes...did she never blink? Abruptly she lifted her head, but in the moment before he turned his away, he saw that she was looking distractedly to one side, listening to an announcement from the platform. The train would take one of two branches at the next station. Sometimes they changed their minds, you had to listen. The doors closed and he hadn't heard. Let it be! If she alighted at the next station, well, he could too! It didn't matter which line he took. They joined up later and he rode on for several stops.

On the second page of the paper his eye was caught by pictures of the war; tanks, explosions, soldiers, the waste sickened him. His eyes felt irritated and smarted as though stung by the desert sand. The whole world gone mad, and for what? Life went on. Take the woman: it was plain to him she was caught up in some close drama of her own – what might it be? By the cut of her clothes she was a well-bred woman. He winced as two lines of thought crossed in his head: here he was, calmly wondering what sort of calamity might have befallen her that she could look so stricken; at the same time, his thoughts were a hotbed of fantasies. He pictured her crossing a bridge in the wind, her dark coat billowing, her hair blowing across her face. For a moment, as his mind focussed sharply on this scene, it seemed unbearable that this woman should be someone he had casually sat opposite not ten minutes ago on a train. How had he worked himself to such a fever pitch in that time? How had the few glimpses of her face worked so powerfully, and stirred such agitation, such peculiar excitement as he was now feeling?

In a moment he had decided: if she left the train at the next station he would follow. He would casually cross to the other branch, as though it was something he naturally had to do. If she crossed too, perhaps they could continue their journey together in harmless, one-sided companionship, in a sort of secret union; it was, after all, harmless and so...harmless...her calves were crossed and elegant in dark stockings, the skirt long, the knees shapely through the light fabric; the train was slowing, he frowned and clutched his paper. Should she move, he must be ready to follow quickly; so easy for a figure to be swallowed in the crowd, the teeming carnival of the underground...

She was not getting off. She was looking above him, her mouth a little open, and he imagined in the brief glimpse he allowed himself that her breath was coming in short gasps. Perhaps she was ill! Again he felt his scalp prickle as he stared intently at the newsprint. He hated illness in public places. But she did not look ill. He was sure she wasn't ill. It was something else. A matter of love, surely, a matter of the heart. In spite of himself, he felt like smiling; a middle-aged gent on his way home from the office, making up stories about a pretty face. Strangers on a train. The doors closed. He really had intended to get off the train if she had! What would he do, follow her? She would have left the station, and then where would he be? Stranded, on the platform, the picture of foolishness. It was not like him to risk looking foolish. In this way, he tried to swallow it down, the rise of his feelings, the lightness that took hold. The next stop was Waterloo: he thought of that picture of the bridge in purple smoke and dusk. She would get off at Waterloo. She would cross the bridge in the evening with the sky and the water turning just those lurid colours: a dark, threatening cumulus of blues and purples.

Far underground, where seven tunnels met in a wide passage, seven streams of people merged and massed at the foot of the escalator. She took the right hand side. She was a swift and accurate mover in a crowd. He trod on toes and elbowed people out the way, distantly amazed at his own rudeness. He almost lost her on the steps behind a group of boys. He almost lost her again passing through the ticket barrier. Caught behind an old man, his impatience turned to panic. There was only one reason he was emerging from Waterloo station at five on a Tuesday and it was itself so elusive he had difficulty keeping it in his grasp. She was slipping away from him. Gritting his teeth, he pushed through the crowd, muttering excuses, his eyes fixed on the black hat thirty yards away. "Alright, alright", the ticket collector said, and an old lady nearby clucked reprovingly.

The black hat was still visible beyond the people walking the long corridor at the back of the concourse. Red railings. White tiles. It was a long time since he had been in Waterloo station. A beautiful building, with its latticework and gables. He remembered it well and knew if he glanced to his right, past the telephones, he would glimpse the lofty iron trelliswork of the roof. She was now turning towards the York Road exit.

His shoes sounded smartly on the tiles and for the length of the corridor he allowed himself to feel as full of purpose as he sounded. In fact, he was in a strange state. His rational side was sitting back, far back in the shadow of this thing, whatever it was, that was driving him forward in her pursuit. Having left the train he knew there was no turning round. The balance tipped, his excitement tampered with the valves of his heart, he was passing through fire. He could just see the tails of her coat billow as she turned the corner. He racked his brains to recall the geography of the place: another flight of stairs and then a confusion of turnings and exits – the red iron gates folded back from the main exit ahead. He would surely lose her there. The humiliation of turning back now! He broke into a heavy run.

It had begun to rain, an unsteady drizzle, and commuters were pouring into the station. By the taxi rank, he stood a moment, out of breath already, searching for her. She had broken free from the crowd and was heading for Waterloo Bridge. Years before, he had worked for a while with the homeless on the Embankment. He and a group of others had brought them food, sat around the fires when they were welcome, listened to the stories. Memories of that time flooded him as he descended to the riddle of subways and emerged on the great bowl, wet now and bleak as ever. She was entering the far tunnel, the one that led up to the bridge itself. To follow her, he would have to pass them, the shambling figures round their fires, huddled in their blankets. Suddenly, he felt his face begin to burn with shame. Once he had come here with time and food to offer the hopeless. Now he hurried blindly across the concrete, his thoughts in uproar. Follow her! Follow her you fool! Soon she will be gone. Soon you will walk by the river, by the Queen Mary and Cleopatra's Needle, to Embankment station to catch the next train; for that is what you are going to do, you sad old man. No more of this. You are a plain man. No more of this madness then. It does not belong in the vessel of your life. It was not meant.

Ahead, he saw them, overcoated men, hanging around by the bottom of the ramp. They watched her pass by, hands in their pockets, and he imagined their eyes, dull and hooded. They let her go by, no one made a move. His face was still burning, though he knew they could not see, and his hands hung stiffly by his side. No time, he muttered to himself as he approached. One of the men moved his hand, scarcely bothering to make a supplicatory gesture. He shook his head quickly. No time now to fumble in pockets for a coin and shrug off the response in a welter of discomfort and shame. She was on the bridge. Let me go now, he pleaded silently to the hunched figures, let me go.

The crowd moved from North to South. She walked by the rails and people stepped aside to make way for her. It was difficult to see distinctly, but he thought that people turned as she passed and he understood this. Like him, they could not help taking a second look. He imagined the whole flow of city workers coming to a halt, piling into one another, trying to turn back and follow her. It seemed as though only he was going in the right direction. I am walking to Embankment station, he told himself, but he knew it was not so. He was following this woman. Something in a stranger's face had made it impossible to remain on the train he travelled on every evening to his home in Woodside Park. He had done something unaccountable; now he felt as though the gesture had launched him into an uninterruptable state. With the wind hitting him hard downriver and the rain blowing on his face, he knew now he could make no mistake. He was carried forward, against the crowd, his eyes continually seeking and finding the woman ahead. He was filled with a sense of irony, but it had no object.

It was simple on the bridge. He even gained on her, making up for the gap that had widened in the station. She was now ten yards ahead, no more. He could see her ankles, the dark heels of her shoes on the wet pavement. Her hat sat crookedly and the wind blew her hair exactly, yes exactly as he had imagined. He laughed aloud, and the sound was carried away on the wind. Now he had a chance to look around him – the vast panorama of the Thames, Westminster to Blackfriars, the proud riverbanks. It was years since he had walked here. He felt tiny. They were all specks, hurrying across this great structure, pendulously draped across the expanse of roiling water. Even the river was tiny, a blue streak on a map, dividing the grey stain that was London. Only she was something, this woman. By her very rejection of everything around her, she became something herself. He was nothing, he knew that, and he did not mind. She was something and he had understood. Now he was allowed to follow her; for a brief span of both their lives he would bind them together. It was irrelevant that only one of them knew. One was enough. And besides, he thought, I'm glad it is me. After all, what if she were following *me* across Waterloo bridge towards the rich promise of the city beyond? I would never have seen those eyes. I would be less than I am.

It remained with him, this inexplicable feeling of wellbeing, all the way across the bridge. Rain was damping his hair down. There were dark streaks on his coat, his briefcase was bubbled with tiny drops. He was able to keep up without effort. As they neared the city side, his thoughts began to roam around the hub of streets leading to Covent Garden and the West End. Still, he did not allow himself to speculate where she was going. His thoughts were dreamlike, everything unpleasant was submerged.

It came as a shock when she made a rapid turn and began to descend to Victoria Embankment. A quick decision was needed: on the bridge, where there were hundreds of people, it was easy to follow her without being noticed. On the Embankment there were few people; he would be conspicuous keeping ten, even twenty yards behind a lone woman. He stopped by the parapet where it curved out to the steps down. She had already disappeared but she would emerge below; he could see then where she went. Once again, he told himself that he was going to walk to Embankment station. His eyes on the dirty blue and white of the Queen Mary, he waited until she would have emerged below. Yes, she was there, heading upriver towards Cleopatra's Needle. The stairs were wet and the passage smelt dank. He could hear the cars passing outside, but for a few seconds he was alone on the staircase, clattering down, his hand out in case he slipped – and she was out of sight. Now, he thought, imagine she is gone. When you emerge, she is nowhere to be seen, the bond is severed and you carry on...as though...nothing...In the moment he reached the street, his eyes sought her avidly. She was still there, crossing at the lights, walking straight in the rain. He followed, grateful, absurdly relieved; happy again.

The gap was wider than ever. He could scarcely make out the details her hair made against hat and collar. Her hands were pale marks against her coat. The lights had changed again and he could have done a dance of impatience as he waited for a break in the traffic to dash across. But there she was, familiar now, he held her warmly with his eyes. He wished to speak to her, silently in his head, but he could find no words. I am here, he wanted to say. Whatever it is, do not despair. But they sounded like the words of a foolish middle-aged man in a mac, and he was no such man. He was nothing.

She was approaching Cleopatra's Needle now, they were rounding the river together, and for the first time her steps faltered. So used to the pace now, he faltered momentarily too. What to do? It was raining: he couldn't sit on a bench, he couldn't stop, it was out of the question. Such an interruption now would lift the lid on a scene of great emptiness. She was walking quite slowly now, with none of the purpose that had carried them across the bridge. Her hands hung limply by her sides. Rain drove in gusts against their faces. He was blinded and he felt at risk. Great peril, somewhere, just behind him, breathing on his neck. Instinctively, he raised a hand to the back of his neck as though to swat a fly and at the same moment she stopped. She had reached the sphinx, the first of the two that flanked Cleopatra's Needle. She put a hand out as though to touch the stone, but it touched nothing. As he watched in disbelief, walking as slowly as he dared now, she turned and descended the few steps to the parapet overlooking the river. Standing there, she put her hands flat on the broad wall. The wind chose that moment for a vicious squall that lifted her hat and carried it in a trice up, somersaulting once, and then swiftly out over the river and down until it was lost from view. She did not seem to notice. He could see one side of her face, close enough now to make out that her eyes were open and staring across the river, wild as they had seemed on the train, staring at his own feet.

There was no alternative. He must pass her by, leave her behind. It never entered his head to do otherwise. But his eyes were fixed on her. If he had to tear himself away, he would see her until the last possible moment. She looked tragic now, standing like that, with her hands spread out, flat on the stone, and her hair blowing unchecked across her face. As he reached the sphinx, once again as close to her as he had ever been since leaving the train, able to make out the curve of cheek and neck, she tipped back her head and shouted. The words were blown to him, fouled by the same wind that carried them. He made out sounds, sounds only, they made no sense. For a blind moment, it occurred to him to stop, approach her, touch her shoulder. As soon as it was conceived, the idea of intruding on her distress revolted him. Turning his collar up, he began to walk quickly, past Cleopatra's Needle, past the second sphinx, up the bank of the Thames River towards Embankment station.

Before the bridge he crossed and entered the station in a crowd of others. Through the ticket barrier and down, mechanically following the black arrows. All at once, he was on another train platform, waiting in the close air for another train. On the surface, his thoughts were childishly simple. He observed several things: on the opposite platform, a man shook out his umbrella with a grimace. A child skipped close to the platform edge. He felt the need to urinate. Deep in his brain, the sounds he had heard were being swapped and juggled, echoing in patterns that veered close to sense, then back to unintelligible sounds. But before the train reached the station, while it was still rumbling through the dark, something clicked and he could clearly understand what she had said. The headlights were visible now and a grubby wind blew. They were suddenly obvious, the words, and he felt momentarily exalted. Turning a little, catching the last moment of quiet before the air filled, he began to say them over and over, softly, to no-one in particular.

The Catch

Eamon, Rory and the other mermen were all in The Fish
Bar in Clontarf by 8 o'clock Friday as arranged. The last
to arrive was the Birthday Boy, and when he did there
were grunts of surprise among the lads. Billy
approached their table rather awkwardly:

"Er – lads, meet the maid."

Helen smiled at the company and nine pairs of
merman eyes rested on her long slender tail as she
tucked it gracefully in under the seat beneath her.

"Gentlemen," she said quietly.

Billy, rubbing his hands nervously, seemed to think a
little more explanation was in order. After all, few of the
men were ever seen in public with their maids, except at
church, or similarly boring parent-teacher meetings
they were forced to attend.

"Uh – she's learning to drive," he nodded in the
direction of Helen and winked with the other eye.
"Thought I'd give her a bit of practise."

"Ah Billy now," said Joe, "I thought I heard you'd a bit
of an old smash-up in the motor. Brought her up on
some rocks didn't you?"

"Yeah, well," Billy looked round defensively, "She was
an old wreck of a boat. I only used her for getting me
home. Redrock's a bitch to negotiate in rough
weather..."

"What's your Birthday poison?" cut in Michael and
Billy got up gratefully to follow him to the bar.

"I'll help you Mick. Ten pints of winkles" he told the
barman, "Oh, and a crab claw for the lady. 'Cos she's
always crabbing at me," he added with a nudge and a
wink to Michael, who chuckled appreciatively and
turned to the corner where the lads were.

"Great tail on her though," he said.

"Yeah," said Billy, sulkily. He was thinking of Helen standing in the hall, dressed to go out, refusing to let him go alone. Thinks I can't drive with a few pints on me, he thought bitterly. I'll drive *her*. The shame of it! Still, she had a great tail. And her voice wasn't bad either, when she sat like that on the rocks at the Bailey, combing her hair – if only she'd do it more often instead of wasting her time with this degree business.

Conch-bloody-ology! What more did the maid need to know about shells, for crying out loud? The world was full of them. Shells shells shells, for breakfast, dinner and tea. He planted three pints of winkles on the table in front of his mates and pushed the crab claw across to Helen. She raised her eyebrows but said nothing. In fact she'd said nothing so far this evening. As soon as Billy had gone to the bar, an awkward silence had fallen punctuated by snorts of suppressed laughter and the occasional muttered comment. Now the merman next to her pointed to the crab claw and cleared his throat.

"Into crab, then?"

"Well, I'd normally have something a little stronger, but I'm driving."

"Right. Who's looking after the kids tonight then?"

"Dermot. Our eldest. He's sixteen now and we trust him."

"Haven't you a daughter not much younger?"

"She's out tonight. They take turns."

Rory shook his head. "Mark my words, you'll regret that," he said knowingly. "Give the girls ideas and they'll never lift a finger for you again. Sure give the lad his bit of freedom, wouldn't you?" "Hey Rory!" someone called from across the table, "Where's the maid tonight?"

"Oh she had a pressing engagement," Rory grinned, "with the ironing!"

There were roars of laughter. Helen was studying the tiny whorled shell he wore in one earlobe. Pearly nautilus, she thought, a cephalopod mollusc. From the Greek *nautilus*, sailor, and *naus*, ship.

Three pints later the mermen were swapping jokes.

"What's the difference between a Northsider and Batman?" said Greg, who liked to frequent the waters round Killiney. "Batman can go into town without robbin'!"

Several heads at the bar turned.

"What does a merman in Dalkey say to his boss at the end of the day?" countered Billy. "Night da!"

The twins from Baldoyle Flats slapped their tails appreciatively.

"Hey! What does a hungry merman do when his wife won't cook dinner? He batters her!" There were cheers and roars of drunken laughter. Helen took her bag and slipped off quietly to the Maids' room. In the mirror, she ran a hand down her thick glossy hair, remembering the time she had suggested to Billy that she cut it. It slows me down, she explained. Billy had been livid."Cut your hair? he'd screamed. What would you have to comb while you sang to me?"

In the end, she had come round to his way of thinking, but only because of the singing he didn't know about – her secret nighttime journeys to the Kish lighthouse where she sat for hours on the rocks, combing and singing away the sorrow of the day. Billy only knew about the regular everyday singing that she did to please him – the soulless stuff, the type of songs fewer and fewer mermaids were content these days to sing for their men.

She leaned forward to the mirror with her hands on the rim of the basin and looked herself intently in the eyes. Helen, she said to herself softly, sing your *own* song.

The Fish Bar finally closed its doors at midnight and the mermen stood around outside, some with half a pint of winkles left, which they knocked back in one to the whoops and jeers of the rest. Billy stood with a hand on the window to steady himself and belched generously.

"Have you the keys," said Helen quietly to him.

"Night Billy! Hope your birthday finishes in style!" shouted Joe.

"Whoah there boy!" Eamon gave Helen a pat where tail

met waist. "Night now!" he winked at her. She turned coolly back to Billy. "Come on Billy, the keys." "Ah now – I'll be fine taking her out into the harbour!" he said loudly. "You can bring her round the rocks if you like," he finished in a savage whisper to her.

"Thanks, I'll swim," she answered and began to make her way to the harbour wall where men were calling goodnight and getting into boats.

"Helen – wait!" Billy followed her angrily and put his arm roughly round her shoulders. "Come on. You're getting in the boat with me." He pressed the keys in her hand and waved cheerily to the lads who were making catcalls. "Sure she's getting the hang of it fine," he said to the man in the next boat as Helen sat into the driver's seat. "I just like to give her some practise." Helen, who had been driving for eighteen years, guided the boat expertly out from among the others and cruised gently in the direction of Howth. By the time they rounded Red Rock, Billy was noisily returning winkles to Dublin Bay.

Nothing marked the spot. Some families liked to mark their homes with a buoy or a rock if they were close enough inland. Helen had always been proud of her skill in diving at exactly the right spot and Billy, for once, had respected her wishes. It meant he could occasionally lose his way coming home and stop over at Kathy's place, which was unmistakeably marked with a shining red buoy.

Helen cut the engine and let the boat glide to a halt. They sat in silence for a few moments, looking at the lights of Dublin in their lovely horseshoe. "Jeez it's lovely," said Billy, a little tearful after the journey. Helen said nothing. "And you make it lovelier," he said awkwardly, placing a hand on her tail, and hiccuping softly. "Shall we go down then love?"

They slipped over the side of the boat and, their tails making perfect figures-of-eight, swam into the deep.

An hour later, Billy sleeping deeply, Helen finished up some study and looked in on the kids. She stood at her bedroom doorway for a while, looking at her husband.

"Happy Birthday love," she whispered and then set off, swimming north, close to the surface until she could see the searchlight through the moonlit water. Just northwest of the Kish was her favourite rock. She found it effortlessly and sat for a while breathing the salty air. A slight wind lifted the sea and sucked it back down the rock. Her hair was freed from the water and, lifting the comb to it she began to sing. There were no words, but no mermaid hearing it could fail to understand and be moved to join in with her own wordless song. She sang from her heart and bones the heavy burden of the day, the same sorrows and secrets, the hidden pain she sang to ease every night. I have this, she was thinking, I have this and no-one can take it from me.

A mile away, a Howth trawler rocked gently in the swell and two fishermen sat smoking on the deck.

"I sometimes think, Paddy," said one, "that even out here in the middle of bloody nowhere, the wife won't let me alone."

"How's that?" said Paddy.

"The wind. Listen. It sounds like her singing in the bath." The two of them laughed heartily and went below deck for the night.

The Night Before

The knock on the door. I drop my knees from their hunched position and try to relax, to shake off the web of thought the quiet was spinning. I call out Come In and he enters smartly. There is no pretence.

"Hello."

"Hello." I don't want to call him Captain. It's ridiculous. Yet I don't feel like the intimacy of first names.

"I saw the light was on, so I took you up on your offer."

"Yes. Sit down." I move the papers on my desk. He takes in my books, the letters, the photographs and few pictures I have in a brief sweeping glance; crosses his legs and offers me a cigarette. The light prickles at his moustache. As I lean forward for him to light my cigarette, I want to say something to disperse the light dust the movement disturbs – that timeless moment of sexual promise.

"I wouldn't have thought they'd let you keep a moustache like that in the army."

"Oh the 'tache," he strokes it. "Yes well they've tried, but I just tell them they're wasting their time."

He's so self-assured: he speaks quickly and without smiling. I noticed it the afternoon we found ourselves lunching across from one another in the mess tent. An air of dismissiveness. It aroused in me the urge to prove myself, an annoying tendency to be on the defensive. There's nothing to prove, I tell myself firmly.

"Don't you sleep?" he says.

"Not very well. Sometimes not for a few nights running, and then I need a whole weekend."

"Yes. I haven't been sleeping well lately." He says it so

matter-of-factly that I wonder whether in fact he has just dropped by for some night conversation. Is it going to be a session, I wonder, a long night.

"Nightmares?" I ask casually.

"No. I don't suffer from nightmares." He takes a long drag. I notice with surprise that his hand is shaking, almost imperceptibly. "Just insomnia. It's this bloody...quiet."

"It's better than rain."

He looks at me with an expression I can't fathom.

"What brought you here, if you don't mind my asking?"

"No. It was a mistake." I laugh. "Well, chance I suppose. I don't want to ruin my credibility."

"Oh I think your credibility is quite intact. That was quite a little talk you gave the first day." He stubs his cigarette out and I try to quell the flurry of irritation that his air of superiority causes me. I hesitate, unsure of how to answer. Then, as if aware he has rubbed me up the wrong way, he adds: "Don't worry. I'm a gentleman."

For some reason, this increases my irritation.

"Why have you come to see me?" I try hard to sound neutral, unchallenging. Remember what you are, I tell myself. Remember what you're here for. He smiles for the first time.

"Conversation. I'm bored."

It's a good try, but I'm not fooled. In fact, at that moment I am suddenly convinced of something, and I feel calm. I feel relaxed and willing to let the twists untwist and the sudden corners test my skill.

"Sure. It must get boring, all this waiting around."

"You're not bored, I take it."

"No." I smile ruefully. "War takes care of that."

"How did you get over here?"

"You want the story?" He makes a non-committal gesture, so I settle in my chair and start telling him about My War. It's a story everyone has rehearsed, a conversation piece for rainy nights in the middle of nowhere, hot afternoons hanging round mess tents. It's an easy way to pass the time and I sense he wants to hear it for precisely this reason.

He is listening, his intelligent eyes wandering round the room, but his sporadic questions reassuring me he hears what I'm saying. Nevertheless, I detect a growing unease in him. He smokes heavily, grinding the cigarettes out with increasing vehemence, shifting frequently in his seat. Once, his hand passes over his forehead in a gesture so plainly agitated that I break off what I'm saying and lean forward a little.

"What's the matter, Lewis?"

"What?" He is surprised, then lets his hand fall to his chest where he fiddles with a button of his uniform. "Oh. I dunno. What time is it?" he asks suddenly.

"I don't have a clock. Oh, wait a minute – I've got my little alarm." I get up but he motions me back.

"No, it's alright." There's a pause. "I know the time."

He says it in a low voice, quite unlike his customary tone. I wait for him to go on. When he doesn't, I repeat my question, trying to sound as casual as I can.

"What's the matter?"

"Oh, it's something -" he fishes in his pocket for a cigarette. His hand is shaking visibly now and he fumbles with the packet, making an exclamation of impatience. "There's only one left."

"It's alright. I've got plenty." I cross the room to the bed-roll and root around the pile of discarded clothes for a pack of cigarettes.

"You didn't just come for conversation. Did you?" I make it a question, for fear of it sounding like an accusation. He doesn't answer until I return with the cigarettes and light one. I can see him trying to form the right words. It's a struggle for him. He has to overcome some kind of barrier.

"No, not really," he says at last. There is sweat on his forehead. "I wanted to talk to you about...something in particular."

"The reason you can't sleep?"

"That's part of it." He reaches suddenly into his breast pocket and pulls out a wallet. Flicking it open he hands it to me. Inside the cover is a photograph; a young man, late twenties at most. Black hair, and a face striking for its beauty. He is not feminine, but beautiful is still the word that comes to mind. Lewis returns it silently to his pocket.

"A friend?"

"His name was Jonathan."

I nod briefly. "Recently?"

"Two weeks ago. On the last trip." His voice is brusque, almost business-like now. I sense a great effort. A holding back.

"There's nothing wrong with grieving, Lewis."

"I know, I know, it's a natural process," he says quickly. Then – "This was *different*." He cracks, suddenly, an elbow on the table, his face distorting. Human grief: I've seen it so many times, and still it shakes me to my roots. I wait a moment, helpless as ever, then lightly touch his knee with my hand. He flinches.

"Don't -" A sharp intake of breath, and then something I can't make out. It sounded like 'blame'.

"Blame who?" I ask, and he seems to make a considerable effort to draw back, to compose himself. He rubs one eye with a curiously childish gesture, but then takes a deep breath and blinks rapidly. He is flushed, and I can see the colour spreading to the hairline, which has receded. He swallows a couple of times and then reaches for one of my cigarettes.

"May I?"

"Of course."

The first drag seems to steady him. He pinches the match out and flicks it into the ashtray.

"I'm not sure...this is what I want."

I deliberate.

"I think it is," I say at last. "What I mean is, you must have thought about it for a while." He nods.

"So, whenever the right time is, it is still going to be painful."

He smokes on, controlling himself visibly.

"It seems to me, you're going through something in your head, over and over; it hurts a lot, and you get to the same point every time." I stop. "But not beyond."

He nods briefly. It is enough to encourage me to go on.

"Maybe, if you were to tell me the whole thing – that

whole incident – whatever it was, in all its bad details, it might...it's a kind of...exorcism," I finish gingerly. This is delicate ground. "What do you think about that?"

"Mm." He blows a smoke ring. Misery, I think, the man is in misery. This is something serious. My heart contracts and I realise I'm frightened.

"You don't have to."

"I know."

"But what makes tonight any different from another night."

He can't seem to come to a decision. It hurts me, obscurely, seeing this.

"You already put the thing in motion."

Come on, I want to urge him, open that heavy, dangerous door. And at the same time I want to tell the man to take his awful confession somewhere else.

"I'm going to pour us some drinks." I get up and, passing him, put my hand on his shoulder. His head moves slightly.

"No, don't."

I hesitate, behind him now. He leans forward, elbows on his knees, and drops his face in his hands. I come back and sit down. I have to wait for him to begin. There is nothing else for me to say.

"That night," he says indistinctly, "we were under fire almost all night. Just running. Jonathan got hit." He raises his head. His eyes are swimming, but his voice is low and steady. "He was lying in the grass and I went back for him. To bring him back." He shakes his head slowly from side to side and tears slide down the sides of his nose. He sobs once.

"He was dead," I say, and he nods.

"Did you love him?" I ask softly and the words hang in the room, simple and with a single meaning.

He fingers his moustache, wiping the moisture from his cheeks, and clears his throat.

"Jonathan was homosexual. I only found out a couple of nights before...we went on the mission. I don't know if it was altogether a surprise to me, it's so difficult to decide that now. I've thought about it," he brings a hand down his face in a gesture of great weariness, "so much now. Over and over. I suppose it was and it wasn't. Anyway – he was."

"How long had you known him?"

"Four years."

"And you never guessed?"

"I don't know. I don't want to talk about that." He brings his hands together in a deliberate gesture. A muscle in his cheek is twitching in spasms. "It's too difficult, and I'm not clear about it yet." His face distorts again. "I loved him," he says and an exclamation of pain escapes that is more animal than human.

I feel a cold tingle of perspiration sweep up my back and prickle at the roots of my hair. Something ugly is in the room. I have the briefest vision of a bat, hanging, menacing in its stillness, just beyond the glow of the lamp. A quick blink and he is gone, there are only the two of us, sitting opposite and bound by the dark spell that words cast – Lewis weeping quietly into his hands, me sitting rigid, waiting for him to continue. I am calling up the old strengths, the reserves I summon on occasions such as this: professional equilibrium, feminine tact, gentleness. But there has never been an occasion like this: each one is different. Every man has his story, and every one calls for a new skill, a different word. Lewis stirs, gathers his wits.

"Jonathan was a very honest person. I'm presuming he was honest with me as soon as he felt it was necessary. If we'd been back in civilian life, I think it wouldn't have mattered so much, if and when I was told, how we...came to terms with the thing." He looks down at his hands, clenched tightly, the knuckles whitening. He lets them loosen. A man on a high wire stops every few steps. He seems to hover, weightless, the pole quivering, and the audience is still, breath held – then he moves again and a sigh goes up like a prayer.

"The way that he told me struck me even at the time as a sort of – preparation. As if he thought he would die." He looks up, checking I am listening. I see the pupils of his eyes contracting in their glimpse of the light, then he bows his head again. Wind roams the camp. Wind picks listlessly at the litter by the kitchens. A few rats hesitate, sniffing the new air. Then the quiet returns.

"I think he did believe he would die. Of course, we are encouraged not to think along those lines and of course everyone does. But the language spoken here, it doesn't embrace a vocabulary that allows for such things to be expressed. Have you heard it?" He looks up again. "That subtle...something missing – words that no-one says in public. You just don't say them. Even the stupidest, most junior private knows it. You pick it up when you join. Like a badge. Pin it on. There you go." He chews his lip in silence for a little while. I don't trust my voice, and he seems content to have me listen in silence. He moves a little, thinking his way through the hot damp jungle of memory. There are mines along the path.

"Jonathan knew it too and he stood for it. We used to talk, about death, from time to time. I always wanted to more than he, but he would hear me out. I think – I was more afraid of it than him. But his presentiment affected me. The night before we went...out...I was sure as well. That I would die."

He clears his throat and runs a hand through his hair, starting at the forehead and combing back, once, towards the back of his neck.

"I think I'll have that drink now."

"Good idea." I stay sitting for a moment, trying to communicate calm, good sense, whatever is in order. Then I stand and cross the room, into the shadows. "I've no mixers, I'm afraid."

"That's alright."

I find the bottle underneath my clean uniform. Two fingers from the neck, the liquor burns amber, the colour of water over pebbles in a Scottish mountain stream.

"It's just a Scotch. Nothing special." There are two tumblers in the wooden chest, along with some books belonging to some previous occupant. I pour us both generous measures and accept Lewis's offer of a cigarette from my own box without smiling. There is still a film lying over everything in the room, a membrane that any sudden movement or inappropriate gesture would tear. Lewis takes a mouthful of Scotch and grimaces.

"I don't drink whisky very often."

"Nor I."

He wipes his moustache and blinks rapidly a couple of times. "That night, before we went, Jonathan came to my tent."

Oh yes, this is the precipice. Set a ball in motion now and it will start a journey downwards, there will be no interrupting.

"He came...to ask me would I spend the night with him."

"Yes," I say after a pause, because it seems the syllable is needed for him to continue.

"He told me we would both die." He measures his words. No one is heavier or lighter than the next. "I argued for a while, on the side of continuing life. I played devil's advocate, because by then, I too..." he stops. Remember, remember, memento mori. A man confronting the inexplicable life he is still in possession of, the blood that somehow, against the odds, still flows thickly through his veins; the heart that obstinately ticks.

"I spent that night with him." In a room as quiet as this you could sense the change in breathing of a man entering a dream. "We – well, we spent the night together. I thought it would be my last. I really believed," he separates the words, endorsing each one with a slight movement of his head, "it was my last night alive." He turns to me a face clouded with the failure to understand. What went wrong? the eyes beseech me. What cruel hand swooped in and swapped the stones, one white, one black, one Jonathan's, and one for me? Is this how it is determined? Before, long before the bullet lodges in the heart?

"We slept together and we woke together," his eyes have fastened onto mine, I cannot drop my gaze; he seems to hold me there, willing me to stay with him, locked to him like this, as he enters the heart of the matter.

"That day. I can't remember any details. It's all one colour. We were roused at five. I think we were both –

104

dazed. I don't remember saying anything to him, nor he to me. I don't remember speaking..." his gaze wanders a little to the side of me, as though a new thought is occurring, "after the last words of the night before." He swallows and shakes his head once, slowly. The muscle tic starts up in his cheek again. "It all happened very quickly. We were loaded into jeeps. The roads were bad, no one speaking, everyone smoking, thinking, trying not to think. Then...Jonathan...in the grass -"

"Go back Lewis," I reach out, touching nothing, "go back to where the journey ended. You mustn't get ahead of yourself."

"No," he shifts nervously, his eyes darting to one side. In a monotone he continues. "The jeeps stopped, we were told to get out, form lines; we'd been briefed back here, knew the territory, as much -" he stops and swallows again, convulsively. When he starts again it is in a voice so low and desperate it chills the air it touches.

"I just see Jonathan lying in the grass, and, and I'm trying not to run, I'm trying to bend down and see if he's alive. There's blood. So much blood."

A pause. He's shaking now, so much he has to set the glass down on the table and clench his hands in tight fists against his forehead, so he's leaning over, elbows on his knees and I can't see his face.

"The next bit - is bad. It's very bad. I'm angry. I'm looking down at him and I know he's dead and I get mad, absolutely - furious. I -"

"Go on Lewis -"

"I can't -"

Suddenly he's on his knees, reaching for the metal bin below the desk, retching and sobbing. I jump up, momentarily shocked, then kneel beside him, stroking the coarse army shirt, murmuring incoherent words while he is sick, repeatedly, and sobs out words that could never be written down.

At last he straightens, sits up on his hunkers, his face grey and his eyes closed. He is weeping openly, the tears trickling into his moustache, with a kind of hopeless air of accomplishment. It is finished: the dying words of a man on the cross. He has spoken them now. But in the corners of the room, quick in the shadows, the pendulous creatures hang, with membranous wings and hideous blind heads. Lewis begins to rock back and forth, whimpering, his arms hugged tightly around his middle. He leans far over, rocking like this, as though he would burrow, animal, into the earth and bury it there, the awful memory. A slow horror creeps over me, watching this. I am peering at a man's deepest fear, his torment. My impulse is to get up quickly, leave the room – to find a well lit place and sit there in the electric glare letting the light burn this scene from my retinae.

But I am a doctor and I have no right. You have seen worse, I tell myself, closing my eyes and trying to rationalise the man's whimpering; you have seen men with their legs torn off, heads caved in; every inch of a man's gut strewn like so much butcher's waste on the ground. Yes, but this, the other voice says and I open my eyes in spite of myself: this is a man dragged howling through the heart of something no-one understands.

"I don't know where he is," he says suddenly, muffled in his foetal position.

"It doesn't matter." I touch him now, on the shoulder, cup a hand under his elbow. I want him to get up, to sit again, so that he will break out of this sub-human crouch. A man in this position is something less or more than you want to witness.

"Come on, come on," I try to urge him up, towards the chair; he turns towards me, confused. He hardly seems to know what I want of him. His eyes are troubled, he is still somewhere fifty miles away in the wet grass, the mud, running without knowledge of where or why. A shiver of disgust drags his features briefly into a grimace and he grunts, then feels behind him for the chair and half turns his head.

"Would you rather lie down?" I move to help him, as it seems for a moment his legs will not support him if he stands.

"Yes I think so."

Grateful for the opportunity to do something ordinary,

I go to where my bedroll is and begin to unroll it, straightening the quilt and fetching a pillow. Like a blind man, he lets me lead him carefully to the bed where he lies down, on his side, facing away from me. It isn't cold in the room, but he draws his legs up towards his stomach, rucking the quilt with his heavy boots, and clamps his hands flat between his thighs. Like this, then, he lies, and I can see that his eyes are open, gazing straight ahead.

"I'm going to stay over here." I speak neutrally, into the shadows of the wall beyond us both, where the bats glimmer and leer. "I'll be here all night. If you want anything, just ask me, if you want to talk, to sleep, to leave without a word – you must do exactly as you wish. And don't forget – nothing goes beyond these walls. That's my word as doctor, and as friend."

I've been writing now for almost two hours. He hasn't moved. Maybe he is sleeping. At last I feel tired, as though I could close the book and cross the room, remove my shoes and lie down beside him, pulling over us a blanket I will find in the chest. Soon, it is possible, sleep would come; with any luck, sleep without dreams. And perhaps just before sleep, I might reach out and hold the man lying like stone on my bed, hoping that the touch of another human being might give him comfort, remind him he is not alone. Alive, but not alone. On a shelf above the table is a pottery jar. The colours swim down to me and as I stare they get more and more lovely. It is full-bellied and my eyes take it up and turn it slowly, holding it into the light and then down, with the light clothing it. I look into the dark well of it and bury the light.

The Swimmer

Rene told me to leave. "Imagine", he said, "when you are my age, when you are twenty nine and nothing has been done. You have just stayed here all that time looking after us. It's no good," he said. "You should go away and see what happens. If you don't like it, you can come back. But you must go," he said; and he would not look at me.

I had a lot of sleepless nights after that. Real sleeplessness, when I had to slip out from between the sheets because they were like sandpaper against my skin, and the pillow was like a block of pumice. I would put on my dressing gown and go quietly downstairs. The garden was the best place. That summer the grass was longer than usual. It was heavy and sleek with all the rain there had been in June, and it bent over and hung when the dew made it wet and dark. The feeling of the blades against my skin was shocking. Down the end of our garden we had a swing. The grass grew round that, just as long; it was plain nobody used it. In fact, by the time we came to that house we were all too old to swing. Christian went out on the streets with the other kids. Nobody ever played in the gardens.

I could not swing at night. The terrible groaning sound of the iron chain grinding off the top bar would wake everybody and I just could not have them find me there, out at the end of the garden, swinging away in the middle of the night. That would be bad, there would be questions. It was a pity. I used to love to swing when I was small – it was one of the things a kid could do that really meant something. You could see in other gardens, you could tip your body so the swing climbed and the smallest weight here would bring you higher and the smallest dropping back would slow you down. I swung once on a beach by a lake that was so big I believed it was the sea. I was sure I would have everything, it would all come. I thought about this, down the end of the garden, sitting there, hoping the seat would not groan; breathing the garden and the night down all the back gardens on our road. I thought everything over: should I stay or should I just go away come September when the kids in the neighbourhood were going back to school and it was time to do something. If I stayed there would be this, if I went, there would be that. And then Rene. Always, at the end, my thoughts finished up with Rene and I could not think anymore. Then I would go back to bed and hang the damp dressing gown up behind the door and hope for sleep. In the morning, there he was, my brother, his eyes dark wells, the garden beyond the window heavy and wet and green as desire.

One afternoon we waited in his room. Christian had been skipping school again, his first week back, and we were waiting for him to come in. Dad was at the supermarket. I watched a cat on the garden wall.

"Where can he have got to," I said. "He's never this late."

"He's this late when he goes for his walks along the seafront," said Rene. "You knew he did that, didn't you?"

The cat was still, so still he might have been a stone cat we put down there. How come a cat could stay like that on top of a wall, unmoving, looking at something for a minute and a half; then move as suddenly and jump right down into the grass and be off?

"Yes. I knew he did that," I said. "But I don't know what he's thinking of."

"You know better than anyone," Rene said, and then we left the matter alone because daddy got back. I put the food away and Rene stayed in his room, waiting for Christian to come home. He came back while we were eating, dropping by the kitchen to pick up a pot noodle and a packet of crisps. He was fine, he said, while we all stopped eating and dad fished about in his pocket for his watch.

There was a fight then, about school, and not going to school, and what Christian could expect to get out of his life if he spent a lot of time down in the arcades by the sea-front, dropping money in those machines. Christian said he never went to those arcades, wherever they were, and dad could just get off his back, because he was always down on him and it wasn't fair. And here, he used a swearword under his breath. Dad left the table then, and Rene broke in and spoke to both of them, trying to stop the argument.

I don't know what made me choose that moment to say I planned to leave for London in a week, but it was a bad time to choose and I felt that almost at once, when daddy and Christian stopped arguing and there was dead silence. For a few minutes I was surprised and pleased that such a decision had been reached with so little trouble. Then daddy said, "We don't have to talk about this now honey." The gentleness in his voice made me want to hide away somewhere; to get up and leave the house and go out to a place in the mountains and sit there in the quiet. "We can talk about it later," he said. "I want to sort your brother out here. I believe we have some thinking to do, all of us." Then he sat down in his place again and everything was silent. "Does anyone want some of the trifle I made," I said, but no-one did.

That evening while dad was in the kitchen having a talk with Christian, I sat in Rene's room and we watched TV. While we laughed at a Laurel and Hardy film, a deep loneliness came over me. There we were, I thought, it seemed like yesterday, the three of us and mum and dad. There we all were – Rene with his hands on my shoulders, and Christian six years old and fair as a little Finn; mum and dad looking terribly young. It seemed very hard that you grow up and leave, and in the end you only come together for death or marriage, and the cogs grind on one more notch each time until life winds down. Look at dad, I thought, he's fifty-four now and a widower for more than ten years. The room was suddenly a strange place. Life was too big and I

wasn't enough to fill it. For a while I felt the walls
shrink away and although I clung very tightly to myself,
there wasn't enough and I was cold.

When the film was over we sat on, watching somthing,
as though we were frozen there and watching television
was the only thing there was to do. Finally, Rene stirred
and cleared his throat. Don't say anything to me now, I
begged him in my head, please don't say anything. He
asked would I make some coffee for us; but we had
forgotten daddy and Christian in the kitchen. Daddy
wouldn't appreciate me making coffee while he was
giving Christian a 'dressing down' as he liked to call it,
because Christian would take the opportunity to ask me
for support.

"Are they still in there, d'you think?"

"It's been ages."

"It's going to take ages," I said gloomily, and I sat
down again. Neither of us wanted coffee. Rene turned
the TV off abruptly.

"We need to talk about this then," he said. "What are
you going to do?"

I said I was going to London, to stay with Uncle Hugh,
and find a job.

"When are you going," he asked lightly.

It was frightening, coming down to days and dates like
this. I wanted someone else, someone able, to step in
and organise everything.

"Next Tuesday," I said, still thinking: it doesn't have to
be.

"You'd better give Hugh a call."

He put a finger on my wrist and when I met his eyes
they looked tired and strained.

"Have you thought it out?"

"No Rene, I haven't thought it out." I stood now. "I'm
going, but I haven't thought it out. I'll go over and try to
get a job, that's all." The words hung bleakly between
us. How do people live their lives, I thought. Is this it? Is
this how the decisions come about? "And if I don't like
it, after I've given it time, I'll come back," I finished
lamely. He nodded. I wanted to kneel, in my favourite
position, with my head on his lap, with him stroking my

hair. We had sat like this many times, while things were said and not said. At the same time, I knew if I did this now I would get very sad, and I didn't think that would do any good. Instead, I said I was going out to the back room to read. Rene said he thought he would go to bed, he was weary. He used that word, and I knew it did not mean tired. He looked weary and he moved wearily. "Come and see me before you go to bed," he said, as he had said a thousand times. These were the best times, the hour together at the end of the day. "I won't wake you if you're asleep," I said.

Beyond the kitchen, previous owners of our house had built a glass porch. The back door to the garden was there and the room had rush mats on the floor and an old couch and two fraying wicker basket chairs. One wall was lined with bookshelves. The place was always full of junk. But you could sit there for a whole day. It was dark now and chilly. I sat with my legs drawn up on the couch. After half an hour or so, I could hear daddy in the hall, calling my name. He went upstairs. I turned the lamp on and after a while he came back down.

"Hello there," he said, sitting in one of the wicker chairs. "So this is what you're up to."

"Nothing much," I said, embarrassed suddenly.

He sighed and sat back in the chair, making a steeple of his fingers. It was very quiet out there, at the back of the house.

"Have you thought about going?" he said.

"Yes, I've thought it all through," I said. "I think I have anyway," I added, and he smiled. "I'll stay with Uncle Hugh till I get a job and then I'll get a place of my own."

Daddy nodded. "You don't have to go, but of course if you want to you must." His tone was even, as always, the sentence balanced so I couldn't guess what he wanted. There was no use asking.

"Christian will be alright," I ventured. "He looks after himself anyway. Maybe he'll pull together a bit more if he doesn't have me to pick up after him."

He sighed. "Christian," he said. We sat a while longer, talking about London, and then he got up and said it was time for bed. I said yes, but I stayed on after he had gone upstairs, finally switching off the lamp and sitting there in the dark. All the lights were out now. After a while it was difficult to move, almost impossible to think of getting up and climbing the stairs to bed. The strangest thoughts come to you, sitting at the back of your house in the dark, the middle of the night. At last I stirred, as though coming out of a long dream. In my head I had been through all the people I knew, and said goodbye to them. Only Rene remained, on the outside. He would not come in to the group as I said my goodbyes. He waited apart, until the end. If I turned to him, even after they had all left the dream, I knew he would not speak.

The week went quicker than most. It was exciting – friends dropping by, and some nights in the house that were like a kind of festival. At night when I lay awake and the bedclothes were a deadweight, I did not go down to the garden any more. The still swing and the cats rubbing black against the dark brought on a kind of aching in my throat. The night before I left, some people dropped in to say goodbye. There was quite a party in the house, and I sat with my legs tucked under me and my heart numb. It was hard to keep talking to people with my eyes on their faces and my sentences connected to one another. To everyone, I gave the same story. I could stay with my uncle for a while, then once I had a job, I'd get a place of my own, maybe with friends. There were always plenty of people to turn to in London, and yes, I was sure everyone would cope very well without me. Daddy poured drinks and now and then I caught his eye and knew he was watching me in this new light. "She'll do fine," he was telling everyone. "And if she doesn't like it she doesn't have to stay." We were both using the words to hide behind. It was easy to tell our little stories. People knew what to answer. But Rene said nothing. He said more than nothing, I could read his eyes. I'm sorry, he was saying. There is no help for this.

I dreamed I was swimming. Out against the small choppy waves. The wind was warm against my face, that quick wind that came up in the early evening. The boys were shouting from the beach, I could hear them, but I was swimming and swimming, through the deep blue, over to the other side. Maybe they're calling me back, I thought, but the swimming didn't leave much time for thinking. Maybe I should look back, I thought, or maybe I can just keep swimming, over to the other side. After that I thought nothing at all. I just swam.

I saw red, then white, and the flickering of the sun through trees along the sides of the track. For a while, when the train left the port, I hadn't been able to keep still. I had spent the ferry crossing by a window watching the sun on the foamy trail the boat carved in the sea. When the train moved out of the station, I wandered down the swaying carriages; past the first class compartments, down the side of the carriage, close to the windows, so that when the ground fell away and we crossed high over a river, I felt suspended, way up there with nothing below my feet. It was a dangerous feeling and I half relaxed into the danger as though it was my only friend. I stood some more looking out at fields and hills and nothing beyond. Then I returned to my seat and fell asleep there. Now the train was sliding between giant blackened walls and there were four tracks on either side. Trains went by, picking up speed, and we passed some slower ones; there was shunting and smoke being belched out into the heat. It was half six when we shuddered to a halt at the platform. Sun came through the sooty air high up in the station. It's like Dickens, I thought. I tried not to look down the platform to see if Uncle Hugh was there. I didn't want him to be there – I hoped he was still at work, or travelling home on the tube. He hadn't said he'd come. Just that he got home every evening at seven. Hurriedly I scanned the faces, and then walked up the ramp and into the station concourse. So much crowding and noise. I let the crowds dull my thoughts, I let them trample down my rising heart. I don't have to stay here, I thought, and at once I was sure I would not. I can stay a week, a month, and then go home. It's a holiday. It doesn't matter. I'm just coming over for a little while and then I might stay on. Or I might go home.

Harrow and Wealdstone station was nearly in the country again. Hugh wasn't on the platform there either, and I passed relieved through the ticket gate. There was a low stone wall with a stile over it, like the countryside, but across the road some ugly houses and behind them a block of flats. In a grocery store I stopped and bought a bottle of wine. I wanted to start off in the right way with Hugh. He had always treated me like his kid niece. He was the kind of man who was out of touch with kids, who brought clothes two sizes too small for us all, and roller skates when roller skates had long gone out of fashion. It was necessary to show him I'd grown up. I'd left home. Though I could go back. I turned onto his street, nervous now: if only I'd had friends to come to instead of an uncle I hardly knew. And a bachelor. He'd be feeling awkward too. He'd been over-enthusiastic on the phone. I felt the familiar tug: turn back! You can go back now! None of this has to happen! It was terrible, a moment of wanting desperately to turn around and go back. I bit my lip hard, my hand on the gate. The garden was a mess: grass uncut, dusty weeds everywhere. The red paving tiles were cracked, some of them were missing altogether. There was an old milk carton lying by the wall. For some reason, this shabbiness gave me comfort. I bet the gate squeaks, I thought. I bet the doorbell doesn't work, I bet Hugh doesn't know what to do when he opens the door, and he gives me a clumsy hug and we both talk together and stammer and get embarrassed. That's ok, I thought, that's how it'll be. No more thoughts of going home now. It takes time to settle in to a new way. It just takes time. I felt choked in my throat then, and as I opened the squeaky gate and pushed it shakily behind me, I fought back ordinary tears.

Hugh already had a bottle of wine in the fridge. There was some brie cheese and some strawberries, looking unfamiliar beside the milk and bread and sausages. There were potatoes boiling and something else in a pot that smelled like fish. The kitchen was shabby, like the garden: the whole house was the house of a bachelor. It made me feel comfortable, and a little bit sad. I felt a rush of affection for my uncle as he moved about preparing the meal, asking me questions about the journey, and fussing a little in his nervousness. I didn't feel like crying anymore. I was too busy taking in the strange feel of the house and trying to make my arrival a little easier for Hugh.

"How's your father," he said, with his back to me at the sink.

"He's ok. You know dad. I wasn't sure if he wanted me to go or not."

Hugh turned round. "He wouldn't want you to leave," he said, surprised.

"No, that's not what I meant. Just, you know, whether he thought it would be good for me or not."

"Is that why you've come over?"

I thought for a moment. "It's one of the reasons."

"And how is Rene keeping?"

"Fine. And Christian is playing truant to his heart's content."

Hugh chuckled. "Is he now."

He turned out two huge salmon steaks on plates and then some giant potatoes, boiled in their jackets, and peas.

"A no frills meal," he said. "Are you drinking wine now?"

After a few more questions, we ate in silence for a while.

"You'll find it a little simple here" Hugh said suddenly. He poured some more wine. "I mean not all the comforts you're used to, maybe."

"Having no woman in the house always shows," I said, and then wanted to bite my tongue.

He blushed a little.

"You don't need to worry Hugh," I went on quickly. "There's nothing you need to get specially for me. I mean, I don't want anything to change for you. I won't be here long." I was going to add I'd be finding myself a place, but I didn't say it.

"You're very welcome here Camilla," he said, using my

full name to my dismay, as though to assure me he really meant what he said.

"Thanks. Here," I pushed my plate towards him. "My mother told me always to finish what was on my plate, but I'm full and you look hungry."

We finished the bottle of wine and then Hugh said, "Will we open the other one?" He looked at me solemnly, then smiled with such an air of conspiracy that I laughed out loud.

It was not what I was expecting. We moved from the drab kitchen to my uncle's back room. This was where he lived. I imagined brief, distracted forays out to cook the evening meal or make some cocoa at bedtime, then back to his books or his papers. I wondered why he bothered with the house at all, why he didn't just rent a bedsit somewhere, and it would be like this room. We sat opposite, in sad old armchairs, the newly opened wine on the table. There was an unmistakeable air of complicity.

"Your father's bound to ring," said Hugh, and he raised a glass, smiling broadly. "Here's to your arrival in London Town." He was different in this room with all his things around him in a comfortable mess. The shelves were groaning; the motes of dust caught in the evening sunlight. I felt like we were hiding out.

"I don't think he will," I said. "Daddy doesn't fuss."

"He might be waiting for you to ring him."

"No." I thought, if I ring now I'll cry. I'll go home tomorrow. I'll hear his voice and it will be three hundred miles away. "I'll ring tomorrow."

"Do you play backgammon?" he asked suddenly.

We got out the board excitedly. "It's ages since I've used this," he said. I thought of us as kids, unpacking the decorations for the Christmas tree.

"I have to be black," I said. "This way." I set it up so we were playing anti-clockwise towards ourselves. "Sorry," I smiled at his expression. "That's the way I have to play."

"Your father always made me play his way," he shook his head. "I guess he's taught his daughter how."

For a while we played quietly; the pieces clacked softly on the board.

"Got you," he said, or, "This is rigged."

"I don't believe it. Twice double sixes. Have you a secret?"

"I'm a lunatic, I know it," I said, leaving three pieces open to catch him. When he threw the dice then we both laughed out loud. After that we kept up a running conversation, laughing and kidding each other.

"Uncle unused to wine," he said, when I took my last pieces off the board. "We have to finish this now, Cam." He held the bottle up. It was a deep red. We nodded gravely to each other. Yes. Couldn't leave it in the bottle.

"My tongue feels funny," I said as I set up the board.

"Marquis's son unused to wine," said Hugh. "Let's have some cellos."

The records were stacked dangerously in a corner. There was a jar of pickled onions on top, which he carefully laid aside. I watched him lift the needle and place it on the record. He squinted a little through his glasses; now the wine is over, I thought, and it'll get late and we'll have to say goodnight soon and then up to bed. It's a little square room up there. Little white bed. Plenty of dreams in that bed. Don't want them. No dreams tonight, thanks.

"Your go," I said to Hugh. He threw a four and a six.

After some games of backgammon and two sides of the cellos, he asked if I was tired. It was dark and he had lit the lamps, softening the room. I said no, I didn't want to go to bed. "I'll be lonely," I said simply. He nodded, and said nothing.

"You haven't said that the last time you saw me I was sixteen and still at school," I said, smiling.

"I'm not a very good uncle, then."

"No. You're supposed to say 'It seems like yesterday you were only this high!'" I held my thumb and forefinger an inch apart.

"Well," he rubbed his glasses on his sleeve and blinked. "I don't know what nieces are supposed to say."

"Don't they...I don't know, borrow money all the time? And ask for things their dads won't let them have?"

We made some more stabs at being a niece and then fell quiet. I curled up tighter in the armchair.

"These are comfortable. Do you live in this room all the time?"

"Yes. I suppose I hardly use the rest of the house."

I held the inevitable question back, suddenly shy. We had spent a couple of hours hilariously, like old friends. Now I hardly knew what to say. It had not been as I expected, but now that I thought about it, I wondered what I had been expecting. There hadn't been much thinking – not of what would happen after...after I boarded the ferry. Thought had stopped there.

"Can I look at your books?"

"Of course."

Hugh read his paper, while I clambered around the stacked papers and piles of magazines, craning to make out titles. I saw a complete set of old Penguin Graham Greenes. There was an old, old copy of Alice in Wonderland, and one of Dubliners. He had diaries and biographies, war journals – Samuel Pepys, Churchill, AJP Taylor. I stayed quiet, more and more impressed by what I saw, and what it told me of my uncle. But a man's books are part of his privacy. It is a delicate thing to remark on what he reads. I picked out some of them and flicked through the pages. This was out of curiosity: I wanted to see if the title pages were inscribed. I looked for women's names. As long as I could remember, Uncle Hugh had never been mentioned in connection with a woman's name. Inside Faulkner's "The Sound and the Fury", I found my mother's handwriting. To Hugh, she had written clearly, On your eighteenth birthday. I put it back, obscurely ashamed.

"You can borrow anything you like," Hugh said from behind his paper.

"Great. I will."

"Do you read much?"

"Does the Pope wear a funny hat! I couldn't bring many books though. You know, moving round and stuff."

Hugh said nothing. I chose a Graham Greene and settled back in the armchair. After the first two pages it was hard to concentrate above the scenes forming in my head. The blue flicker of the television on the walls of

Rene's room, the warm night drawing the tails of the day through the air down all the back gardens on our road; the swing, hanging straight down. Daddy reading a book in the back porch, his glasses slipping a little too far down his nose. Long fingers. Daddy had shapely hands. That's where Rene got them. And Christian. I wondered if he'd been to school. Do go to school, I had said to him the night before. It was the first time I'd ever broached the subject with him and that was all I said. The less words spoken, the more likely they are to be remembered. Long goodbyes get swallowed up. Quiet words, brief, simple words are remembered and remembered and remembered.

I began to read again, to shut the avenues off, to close down thought and memory. It was a routine I had plenty of practice with. Fly away memory, fly away grief. Before the tears began, I slid off the chair and said "Goodnight Hugh." I was almost past him when he lowered the paper and turned his head. He almost caught my eye, but perhaps he saw my face: raising the paper again he said "Goodnight Cam" in a kindly way. Goodnight Cam, goodnight Cam, I said over and over as I climbed the stairs to my room and the small white bed.

"Cam? Are you alright?"
"I keep dreaming."
"I know. You always will. Where are you? Are you ok?"
Unbearable, the even tone he used, because I was phoning him in the office.
"Yes."
"Where are you? Shall I phone you back?"
"No – I don't know. I'm in some square. Don't phone me back Rene. I'll call you from Hugh's tonight. I just – I'll call tonight, ok? I'm fine now, I promise."
"Alright. Phone tonight then."
"Yes."
Before I put the phone back on its hook, he said, "Be strong."

London was abominably hot. I had to keep getting out a big unwieldy map on Oxford Street to get to the agencies

I'd copied down from the telephone book. I felt unwell and my head throbbed. In the first agency I filled out forms and took typing speed tests and a test involving sums and spelling. The girl said she'd call me if anything came up and I trailed dispiritedly out. After the third agency I could not go on. I walked down a side street and found myself in a green leafy square. It was quiet there and I went into a phone box and dialled the number without allowing myself to think, or decide what to say. After the call, I stood in the telephone box for some time. No one passed by. The shadows of trees moved on the pavement outside. When I emerged, my t-shirt was clinging to me. Next, I went to BHS and wandered round the food department without buying any lunch. On the street again, I opened the map and looked for Russell Square. Under the agency names from the phonebook, I had written "British Mus. Gt. Russell St. WC1B 3DG".

First of all I went to the Manuscript rooms. Joyce, Woolf, Rilke. An amazingly illegible tract from Freud. The Lindisfarne Gospels. I had to look very long and hard at those, and I began to feel the return of calm. It was an afternoon of collecting. From the vast rooms and galleries, I scanned display cases and chose the things I would keep. Sometimes it was an object; sometimes an anecdote from history. A lion from the tomb at Cnidus. I touched the marble; his face was half gone. 300 B.C. Carthage, the Tower of the Winds, The Temple of Apollo at Bassae and the Temple of Artemis, which was burned the night Alexander the Great was born, so he paid to have it rebuilt. Cowrie shells. Weapons. A shield. A spoon from 6th century Cyprus, arrowheads from Viking Norway. Ivory. A tamarisk wood sickle. In the same case as this sickle there were objects that dated from before recorded time. Just bits of smooth stone in roughly carved shapes. I wanted to look at them and look at them and let the past they'd existed through surround me, and absorb the pain of memory and loss.

Finally, I passed through the Babylonian room. There were the Royal Tombs of Ur and the Chaldees. A deed of sale written on stone in Akkadian. A tiny slab engraved with cuneiform hymns to Inana, goddess of love and war. You see, I told myself, none of it matters. Love and war. It all gets swallowed up. It all ends. The Babylonians had lots of gods and goddesses like Ishtar and Inana, I read. Their sumerian priests made offerings naked. Their trade was largely on water, the Tigris and the Euphrates. The wheel was long known. There were clay nails with a treaty written round the wide end, and spears, long and decorated with silver, and hard, oblong mace-heads. There was a gaming board squared off with lapis lazuli. Maps of the Tombs of Ur showed the great Death Pit where the retainers of A-Kalam-Du were killed when he died so they could go and prepare the way for him in the afterlife. There was a silver lyre with a bull's head and the eyes of lapis lazuli. I stood on the other side of the glass, staring into the bull's eye. It was a dull brown colour. Fishing in my bag for a pen, I wrote in the margin of the museum guide some lines I remembered from nowhere: "They are not long, the weeping and the laughter, love and desire and hate. I think they have no portion in us after we pass the gate."

There was little food in my uncle's kitchen. Some aging tins and packet soups; coffee and cocoa. I dumped a heavy bag of groceries on the kitchen table and read again the note in his crabbed hand that I had found that morning. "Keys. Lock top lock on front door when you go out. Best of luck with finding job, Hugh." His cryptic style was somehow comforting. I looked forward to him coming home. I wanted to cook him my nicest dinner. As I cooked, I thought how lonely it would be to come home alone to this house every night, and I wondered if he had ever brought a woman back here. I tried to picture him bringing her into the back room, clearing papers off a chair for her. He would be anxious, and a little brusque. Try as I might, I could not get the picture clear. Laughing at myself, I said aloud, "I bet I was the first female to sit in that room for ten years."

Hugh was taken aback by the scene in his kitchen. There were flowers in a milk bottle on the fridge. There were chopped vegetables on the draining board and strawberries in a bowl. He stood in the doorway, blinking.

"My word. It's a cookery show."

"Do I have to say that line about a little something I prepared earlier?"

"And flowers." He looked around. "You'll be planting a vegetable garden next."

He left the room and I called after him "We can eat in half an hour."

At dinner he ate hugely. After the meal he sat back, and sighed contentedly.

"Ahh. I never told you that I eat midday."

"You eat dinner then?"

"They've a canteen at work. The food is edible."

"So you never cook."

"Rarely."

"And that was your second dinner?"

He smiled guiltily, and patted his extensive middle. "It all goes into this. Did I see strawberries there somewhere?"

"That was very tasty," he said later. "Let's bring coffee inside."

It was cosy, bringing mugs of coffee into the back room. Hugh unearthed some chocolate biscuits.

"I found them in their secret hiding place," he said, and I nodded knowingly.

"Right. Can't have any old burglar getting at the chocolate bikkies."

We sat in the armchairs and Hugh unfolded his paper.

"Did you have any luck today?"

"Just filled out a zillion dillion forms. And tests. They all said they'd phone me."

"What sort of tests?"

"Typing. Sums. And spelling. How do you spell separate? I can never remember if it's 'a' or 'e'."

"A," he said promptly, opening his paper.

An hour later, when I was deep in Graham Greene, Hugh put his paper down.

"Shall I phone your father?"

My stomach tightened in a double knot. "Ok."

He saw my unwillingness. "You don't want to?" he said.

"It's fine. I'd just like to, you know, have a job and things fixed up before I ring. But I know I should," I added, seeing his doubtful look.

"You know Cam," he said, putting his paper aside, "I hope you'll stay here for a little while."

"In London?"

"I meant here, in this house. I've got the room. I like having you here." He said this awkwardly, and I wasn't sure whether he really meant it or not.

"You won't after a while, Hugh. You're used to living alone. Aren't you?" I realised at once that he would take this to mean I didn't want to stay. I cast about for some way to put it right, but he was already trying to push the subject away, to smooth it over so that neither of us would feel bad.

"Let's ring your father, see how they're doing over there." He reached for the phone, hidden behind a stack of papers. "I bet they didn't eat as well as I did this evening." He smiled across at me as he dialled. I smiled back, waterily, feeling my heart begin to race.

Christian answered the phone. Yes, he was well. Yes, school was alright. And yes, daddy was there, he was out the back somewhere. Then Hugh spoke to dad, a funny gruff conversation I had heard before, with plenty of comments about the pound and interest rates. It was odd and sweet to me, hearing the two brothers, ten years apart in age, having this casual chat, because of me. It was the same gap in age that yawned between Rene and me. Then sometimes, it had seemed like no gap at all.

I talked to dad and told him I was ok, and felt my throat tighten when he said "We all miss you here love" in a voice I was unaccustomed to hearing.

"Yep. I miss you too," I said, wishing he could know the truth. Or some of it, at least.

Rene came on the phone and we both spoke in bright voices as though one of us was ringing the other with good news.

"I'll write," I said, three times.

"I wrote to you tonight," he said. "Just a short letter, really."

"Mm. Good." The ache got worse. Trying to sound normal was worse than not phoning at all. I wanted. I didn't want. I didn't know. I felt Hugh was watching me, even though he'd opened the paper again.

It was an immediate relief to put the phone down, and then at once a terrible loneliness came. I sat completely still for a full minute, then said carefully, "They sound fine."

"Yes."

I stared at my open book, not moving, for half an hour before Hugh folded his paper with an air of finality and said, "I'll make some cocoa. Do you want some?"

"No."

He glanced at me and left the room. Rene, I thought, I can't. I don't want to be here, without you, in this horrible nightmare of loss. I thought a few more things like this, all my confidence, all my reason draining away like blood leaving the heart, until I was down there at the lowest ebb. This is the worst, I said softly, aloud, in as steady a voice as I could manage. This is the worst it can get. Then it gets better.

Hugh came in with two mugs and put one on the table near me.

"Cocoa's very good for loneliness," he said. "Shall we play again?"

After we'd played a quiet game of backgammon, I said, "This is good for loneliness too."

"Winning against your hopeless uncle? I should have thought that was a somewhat pyrrhic victory."

We set out the pieces again.

"Do you think you'll stay in London?" he asked.

"You mean rather than anywhere else?"

"I mean rather than go home." Then he shook his head once. "It's too early to ask this. I should leave you alone."

"I'm not going home."

He nodded, and I thanked him silently for saying nothing more. We played backgammon until it was dark outside. He asked me what I was going to do about finding a job and I told him how the agencies worked.

"I'll get something soon," I said. "It's quite easy."

"That's good."

"You're going to beat me. That's not allowed."

"I'm going to gammon you."

"That's worse. I'm a vegetarian."

"You miss Rene a lot?"

"Yes." There was no warning for this change of subject, and I cast about in my mind for the right thing to say. "We're really close. He practically brought me and Christian up."

"Of course. He's what now? Twenty eight?"

"He'll be thirty on September 30th."

"Really. That long ago."

"He's -" I stopped. I didn't really want to continue. There were times I resented that other people had ever laid eyes on Rene. I burned when a remark was casually dropped about him, especially the most innocent ones. And at the same time,the urge to speak of him was like the itching of a limb in plaster. "He told me I should leave." I finished carelessly.

"Then he was probably right."

"Last night, I thought I'd go home."

"That was your first night. You mustn't be lonely." He said this kindly. Kind Uncle Hugh, I thought. Maybe you really do want me to stay here. Maybe you really wouldn't mind, you're lonely, and you find it nice to suddenly have your niece sitting opposite in the other chair. Making cocoa for the two of us. Dinner cooked in the evenings instead of a solitary canteen lunch. Or maybe you're just being kind.

"I will be for a while," I said, almost believing this now. "Then it will go away."

"You'll make friends here," he suggested, helping to build the picture.

"Yes. And I'll get a bit of money together maybe."

"You could go back to college."

"Mm." I wondered what daddy had told him; how he had put it. On the phone? In one of his minimalist letters. Cam has dropped out of college. I'm sorry she hasn't felt it right to see it through. She seemed to be doing so well, I don't really understand. But, as I have told her, she must go her own way. "Maybe I could," I said levelly. "But I don't think so."

I found work with a law firm, typing up contracts and reports. I sat in a huge third floor room in Bayswater with another girl and we typed reports all day long. Linda was twenty. She had a boyfriend and they went out at the weekends to Camden market and Notting Hill to buy records. I listened politely, but I didn't really want to know. For a while, the business of being in London kept me occupied. I stayed in most evenings, reading or writing letters. Hugh and I ate our evening meal together. Sometimes he worked late or met friends in the city. Sometimes I stayed in town and saw a film or went to a museum. I put off phoning the people I knew. There would always be time when I had some money together, when I had my own place, when I wasn't so tired. Next week.

A week after my arrival I told Hugh I'd seen an ad to share a house in Victoria. I was cooking soup and kept my back to him and spoke so casually it sounded strained. He said "Uh-huh" and left the subject until we sat down in the back room to eat. We'd started eating in there after he confessed to me he only ever used the kitchen for boiling the kettle and washing his clothes. The back room was taking on more than ever the look of a den.

As we sat opposite, spooning soup, and reading, he broached the subject again.

"About your living arrangements."

"Mm."

"I meant what I said about you staying here." He was choosing his words with care. "But I don't want you to think you've got to. If you want your independence, that's fine by me."

"Hugh," I laid aside my bowl and spoon. "You have to convince me you mean this."

He tore off a hunk of bread and wiped his bowl with it, round one side, then back. A thorough mopping job.

Then he munched it slowly, ruminating. Finally he, too, put his bowl aside with a sigh, and sat back comfortably.

"Tired old Uncle likes niece's soup," he said.

We looked at each other gravely, and then I nodded.

"Sprightly young niece likes beating tired old uncle to pulp at backgammon," I said, and got up to collect the bowls. After that, the subject of house-sharing did not come up again.

One evening there was a call from a boy I'd known at home. He was passing through London, he said. Could he stay one night, and he'd be on a plane at eleven the next day. John Curie was a friend I'd made in college and when I thought about seeing him, I was glad. He was a skinny, serious guy with a lot of energy, which he often expended in long intense arguments about whatever topic took his fancy. He didn't care, so long as there was someone to listen and ask questions. He hated keeping still.

"Are you out of college then?" I said, but as I did, I could hear the pips of a public phone.

"No more money!" he shouted. "See you Thursday!"

That evening I asked Hugh could a friend stay Thursday night.

"Sure," he said, and then, "Who is it?"

"Guy called John Curie."

"Uh-huh."

"John Curie Bags Of Fury."

"That's his full name, is it."

"Yup. I knew him in college. He's a furious person. But he's pretty nice with it."

"Must be tiring."

"Being nice? You should know. You're quite nice."

He smiled a little, in spite of himself, and I was pleased. Telling my father I loved him, on the rare occasions I said such things, pleased me the same way.

"Another letter from Rene today," he said.

"Mm."

"That boy writes."

"Yeah. He's good at that. D'you want some coffee?"

I wrote too. At all times of the day or night, any thoughts that came. Sometimes half a page, sometimes ten. But I was struggling. The letters were becoming harder as the edge wore off; as there were less and less things we could refer to in our own cryptic tongue. I told him about my job, but it was without interest I wrote to him of a room and a desk and a view he would never see. I wrote about Hugh. "He's a very gentle, thoughtful man Rene," I wrote. "Sometimes I feel he sees a lot, and knows things you wouldn't imagine. I sometimes imagine he knows, but he doesn't. Daddy and Hugh. They broke the mould when he was born."

John arrived in a welter of disorganised luggage. I met him at the station and he hugged me with unexpected warmth.

"Jesus I'd to leg it for my plane," he said. "They kept the doors open for me while they taxied down the runway. Heathrow's a desperate place. And fuckin miles away. What possesses your uncle to live out here?"

He kept it up till we reached the house, a stream of anecdotes and funny stories about the journey. It wasn't until we were at the garden gate that I asked where he was off to.

"Australia," he said shortly, and we stopped, facing each other, our hands on the gate. "I'm getting out."

"For good?" I asked, expecting him to say 'Well, for a year anyway, to see what it's like.'

But he raised his eyebrows and dropped them quickly. "Fuckin right," he said.

Over dinner John told me and Hugh stories: about people I'd known, and things that happened in college, parties and fights and resits, and the nights before resits, and the nights after. He kept us laughing and after a while, Hugh began to remember his own college days in London in the late sixties. Soon he had us crying with laughter, and we carried on long after the meal was over, until Hugh pushed his chair back and said "Will we go for a drink?"

It was the first time since I'd come that we'd been to the local pub. It was full, people spilling out on the pavements, and Hugh said there was another he knew that would be quieter.

"This is where I used to go with your father," he said, leading us into a smaller pub with a wooden floor and wooden benches.

"This is grand," John said, and ordered drinks. When he brought them back to the table I proposed a toast to Australia.

"Yeah," he said darkly, and we drank for a while in a sudden gloom.

"Did you get a visa," I said.

"It's all organised."

"Do you know people there?"

"Eddie's out there. And Anus."

"Anus?" said Hugh.

"His real name's Fergus," I explained. "But he's a bit of a, y'know."

"Oh," said Hugh.

John changed the subject then and we didn't refer to Australia again until after the third or fourth round, when Hugh got up to leave.

"Aged Uncle Reels Home In Alcoholic Haze" he said, and we wished him goodnight.

"Your uncle's great."

"Yeah. I hardly knew him before, but we really get on. He's let me stay there, now he says I can stay for as long as I want."

"How long's that."

"I don't know," I said firmly.

"What are you up to, Cam?"

"What do you mean, up to?"

"You were always a dark horse. There's lots going on in there, isn't there," he nodded towards my head.

"Too much sometimes."

"What are you doing in a fuckin typing job."

"Typing." The coolness of my answer shut him up for a bit. But he wasn't letting go.

"Why did you leave college like that?"

"I wanted to."

"Before the exams? Jesus, Cam. You would've done brilliant."

I said nothing. The alcohol was working and I didn't trust the looseness I could feel, the rising sense of recklessness.

"Did something happen?"

He was looking at me seriously. There didn't seem any point lying, like there always had been.

"I don't want to talk about it."

"Cam. I'm a dead man."

"What?" I wondered for a moment if he was in trouble with the police.

"You know. Remember in the famine when the ships left for America they'd have an American wake the night before."

"Ah John!"

"I mean it," he leaned forward, suddenly aggressive. "They're dead people back there, all of them, and I'm a dead man. It all starts tomorrow at eleven when I step on that plane."

"So I'm dead too."

"No." He sat back. "You're not dead." Finishing his drink, he got up to go to the bar. "You're just asleep." He smiled down at me then and something indefinable was exchanged in the look. A sense of boundless possibility swept over me as I watched him at the bar. I thought fleetingly of standing beside him, with his arm round me. Then another picture blotted this out, and I got up abruptly from the table and hurried to the bathroom as though a giant bat had folded its clammy wings around me and I had to break free.

We drank till closing time, and John attempted to convince me I should come to Australia. There were jobs there, there was sun and sea and endless tracts of empty land. Imagine the outback, he said. You could to out there and just get lost for a month. And the dance parties. He'd heard about them, in Sydney, where twenty thousand people threw a party on the wharves and just danced and drank and got high for a whole weekend. Imagine it, Cam, he said. And I imagined. "You'd love it," he said, and I shook my head.

"Look," he said, and laid both hands flat on the table. "You're not going back home, right? And you're not going back to college. You're sitting here telling me you want to stay in London and type? You're four times brighter than I ever was."

"That's not true, you just didn't work."

"You're still a bright girl Cam, and you're wasting your time."

I felt the unfairness of it building up inside.

"It's not that," I said hopelessly. The pub was emptying. People were drinking up. A barman came to wipe our table. "Let's go back."

Outside the pub he slipped his arm around me, natural as water. "Let's walk," he said.

"No," I said. "Hugh will be asleep. Let's go back and make coffee and scoff some biscuits."

We let ourselves in, giggling a little at the state of Hugh's garden, and made some coffee in the kitchen without switching the light on.

"Let's see if we can locate the sugar," John said, fumbling around the packets and tins in Hugh's cupboard. We spoke in exaggerated whispers and it seemed tremendously funny every time one of us knocked something over. We carried the coffee, spilling some, out into the hall. But instead of going into the back room, I chose the front. This room was as bland as any unused parlour in a fifties house. There was flock wallpaper and a hideous fireplace. We stood in the middle of the room, taking in the curtains and the fake paintings, and I said "This is sad" and we started to laugh and couldn't stop.

"What the fuck's this?" John held up a plastic vase with a single plastic flower. I exploded with fresh laughter.

"It must have been my granny's. Aw, look at this!" I picked up an ancient magazine rack in the shape of a swan. There was a Daily Mirror from 1989. "I can't believe this! Hugh must never come in here."

"The Room That Time Forgot," said John in a deep voice. More suppressed laughter. We sobered up a little then, and sat side by side on the couch, reading the unlikely news of March 28th 1989. We read our horoscopes, and decided what we'd watch on telly. We started the crossword, then gave up because neither of us wanted to fetch a pen. I lay back on the couch with my legs across John's lap.

"So tell me," he said, and then stared into his coffee cup for a while. "You couldn't take the pace or something. Was that it?"

"It pissed me off," I said, "going in there, taking classes, writing essays. What could I do at the end of it?"

"More than type," he said, barely audibly.

"I'll get a better job," I said, but he shook his head.

"I don't understand you." He was playing with the buckle on my shoes, pulling at it and letting it go. "I never understood you. Great crack to be with, but one move and you clammed up."

I let my head drop back on the armrest so he couldn't see my face very well. It was as though he had me trapped there, gently trapped, like an animal he was holding firmly by the paw.

"Will you sleep with me?"

"No."

"Once. The night before I go, huh? One last night."

"No John."

"Your uncle won't know."

"It's not my uncle."

"Have you ever before?"

"This isn't questions and answers time, John." The blood pumped slower, somehow, with my head at this angle. It rose with effort to the brain and I felt that racy feeling from too little oxygen, that quickening before you take a high dive.

"There's no need to be ashamed of that. I think it's nice."

"You don't know. You don't know what you're talking about. I'm not a virgin." I stopped on the brink. You could dive from here and you might be dead before you touched the water. "Now leave the subject alone." There was a deathly tone of authority in my voice that surprised me.

John said nothing for a time. Then I felt him circle my

right ankle with his fingers. They just met. "I really like you, Cam. If there's something that's happened to you and you think it would help to say it to someone you'll probably never see again, go ahead. I won't be seeing anyone who'll need to know."

Say it then, Cam. Just say the words. Just see what they sound like, hanging in the room here for a while, then going away. Would they go away? They might always be here then, like a murderer's bloody hands, veined and terrible. They are bigger, those words, than this room. Bigger than the house, than London, than the whole of Australia. They're too big for me, and too big for Rene. They sent me away, and I haven't gone far enough.

"Maybe," I said, "I'll follow you out."

I woke early, to sudden, sharp jabs of panic. I lay, not moving, as though the dread were a physical pain I would provoke below my ribs. Sunlight moved in the room. Where did childhood go? Pain of memory...where all the places I loved, where all the people...other people don't get scared like this...it will go away, I know, but it's terrible now...All this before I lifted my head and saw John, head thrown back against the couch, one hand still resting on my ankle in his lap.

"John," I said, and my tongue felt like wool. "You've got to catch a plane."

It was only 7am. We stumbled about, collecting his luggage, then I walked with him to the station. We were both subdued, nursing our heads, wishing we were asleep between cool white sheets. The idea of a journey to Australia was remote as a tiny island in a far-off sea.

"Can't believe it," John said indistinctly as we stood, squinting down the line. It was his only concession to the size of the trip he was about to start. "Put a stone rolling and look what fuckin happens."

I walked to a bench and sat down gingerly.

"I feel terrible."

He shrugged the heavy rucksack off and dropped it beside me with a grunt. We sat in silence till we saw the train, far off, a silver ribbon moving painfully slowly up the track. The approach of the train threw us into an uneasy kind of dither. We stood, and John fiddled with the rucksack, adjusting straps and checking all the zips were closed. I walked down the platform a little way, wishing there was more time, that we had the whole morning to sit and talk it over in a cafe. I turned back to John, feeling an impulse to snatch more time.

"Will I come to Heathrow?"

"To the airport? Why?"

"I want to. I want to talk to you a bit."

He shrugged. "Do, so. It's a hell of a way. You'll be late for work."

"Who cares."

The train was closer now. Caught in the trap of the decision, I had alternate visions of being on the train with John, and of walking slowly back to the house; Heathrow, the bustle of luggage trolleys and flight calls; my uncle's kitchen, quiet except for the hum of the fridge; waving to John at the departure gate; a cup of coffee.

When the doors opened, John put a hand on my shoulder. His face looked grey, strained, even though he smiled briefly.

"Don't come with me Cam. I'd rather say it here, and then I'm off."

"Ok." I smiled too, happily. "I don't mind. It's just – I wanted to talk more. You know, find out things."

"Do you still think you'll come?"

"Yes."

"I'll write to you, tell you how to apply and everything." With his other hand, he stroked my neck gently, twice. "I think it's the right thing."

I looked away, over the roofs of the houses, to the ugly flats beyond. Then back to John, watching me.

"I don't know what's right," I said. "But however far I've come, it hasn't been far enough."

He went then, hauling the rucksack in and leaning it against the carriage wall. He came back out onto the platform and kissed me quickly, on the cheek.

"I'll see you," he said. "Off you go now."

"Write to me and tell me how to get a visa," I said. All the way down the road, I didn't look back, even when I heard the train start up, and it passed me on my right. I just raised my hand once as it went by, in case he was looking.

Hugh's kitchen was terribly quiet. I put away the things from the night before and made myself some tea. Then I brought it upstairs and drank it lying on my bed. It was nearly time to leave for work, but I'd told Linda I might be late, in case I went to the airport. I lay there, hearing front doors slam down the road, and the clink of milk bottles and the squeak of garden gates. Suburban London. It was warm. I sighed deeply. To my surprise and unease, I found myself in a huge enclosure in the middle of a city, with hundreds and thousands of people, all listening avidly to a speaker I could not see. He was persuading them of something. There was a man in white who had lured me there, half against my will, but only half. He stood near me, watching me, smiling. I felt he knew more about me than I liked, and I wanted to go, but I was fascinated. At last I got anxious and knew I had to leave at once. I went to a wooden door in the enclosure and the man in white was there, smiling, opening the door, but inviting, pressurising me subtly to stay. I found myself giving him my address, knowing it was inadvisable, but unable to help it. He took it and said he would most definitely be in touch. I hurried home to a dark, low, green house with many doors and windows I had to open, and a large, wild garden. The men of my family would be home soon; I had to put on lights and prepare food. Rene would be coming home.

That evening I cooked us fish, but Hugh didn't seem very hungry. He sat quietly at the table, and I began to feel alarmed. Maybe he had heard us downstairs – he presumed we'd slept together, and he was angry. Uncomfortable thoughts formed: maybe he was annoyed we'd woken him, or that John had stayed at all. It was awkward. I wanted to talk to him, to tell him, and ask his advice. And now he was strangely quiet like this, I suddenly wasn't sure how to approach him. At last, I said,

"Did we wake you last night, Hugh?"

"No, no," he said, starting from a daydream.

"Were you...angry John stayed over?"

"Angry?" he looked bewildered, and then shook his head, and smiled weakly. "Not at all. In fact," he hesitated, "the truth is I'm not feeling very well."

Relief made me overflow with sympathy.

"Why don't you sit inside and I'll make you coffee," I said, and he agreed. "Or would you rather tea?"

"I thought this morning it was too many beers," he said, when I brought him the tea. "Thank you. So I gave myself a ticking off and trudged into work."

"I didn't feel on top of the world myself."

He sipped some tea and I noticed he was shivering a little.

"Have you got a temperature?"

"I think I'm coming down with flu," he said, and smiled miserably.

At half eight he succumbed and went up to bed. I looked in on him before I went to bed myself. He was alright, he said, which was plainly untrue, and he didn't want anything. I made him take some aspirin anyway. Fetching some water in the kitchen, I thought how bleak his bedroom looked, the nondescript wallpaper, his clothes draped over a single chair, no pictures or signs of someone else's affection or care. While he took the aspirins, I stood uncertainly by the bed, trying not to let my eyes rove round the room. He handed me the glass and wiped his lips.

"You're good to me Cam."

"I'm glad I'm here and you're not sick on your own." I left then, with the thought unspoken between us, the picture of other times when he had lain, sick and miserable, alone in the empty house.

"Poor Hugh," I whispered to myself as I snuggled down in bed. "I hope you won't mind I'm going." I thought a while about the other thing: how close I had been to telling John, how simple it had seemed. I shook my head on the pillow. How awful if I had. I could never see him again. I could never think of going out there. "Never never," I whispered aloud. "You must never tell another soul." I thought about souls then, and wondered as so often before, what it was all about. What was wrongdoing, what was evil, and why; how you were punished. Heaven. Hell. The terrible in-between. Nothingness. I hope there's nothing, I thought. God, let there be nothing, because I don't want to be judged. "Poor me," I said aloud. "Poor me." And then, "Poor Rene."

I had a bit of money of my own for the first time. I took a trip to Oxford Street and mingled happily with the Saturday afternoon crowds. I bought a pair of leggings, and then a large towelling dressing-gown for Hugh. I bought three t-shirts and a book. I agonised all afternoon, wandering in and out of shops, picking things out and rejecting them: finally I bought Rene a globe for his thirtieth birthday. I was able to choose it over the other gifts only because the thought of packing and sending it gave me such pleasure. The postal system was slave to my whim. I'm giving you the world, I thought, as I watched the assistant lower it gently into a box filled with polystyrene chips. It was a beautiful thing.

Back at the house I unpacked my gifts with a thrill of pleasure. I tried on the clothes and then knocked gently on Hugh's door. He was propped up in bed, listening to the radio, and he admired the leggings and the new t-shirts. I tried on each one in turn for him. Then I shyly fetched the dressing gown. He opened it and I noticed his flush of pleasure.

"Want to try it on?"

He was feeling the soft towelling, smiling and shaking his head a little. It struck me suddenly that perhaps this was the first gift he had received in a long time. My father was not an effusive man, and they had few living relatives. I could not remember his birthday. He seemed about to say something. Afraid it would embarrass us both I said quickly,

"Like to see what I got for Rene's birthday?"

I came back with the globe and unpacked it reverently. Hugh was genuinely impressed.

"Cam, it's beautiful." He fingered it, turning it slowly on its brass axis. "Look at the journeys the explorers made," he traced his finger across a line. "Here's Blake. Look, Columbus."

I sat gingerly on the edge of the bed, still aware of a sense of trespassing in his bedroom, and we studied the globe thoroughly. Finally he put it aside, and lifted the dressing gown onto his lap again.

"How are you now?" I asked.

"Well, I thought I might come downstairs and have some soup, but I'm not feeling right enough for that."

"How about I bring you up some bread and butter?"

He looked at me with an indefinable expression. His eyes were a pale blue and I thought they were watering.

"I'll do that," I said quickly, getting up. "If you don't eat it never mind."

"Thank you," he said, when I was at the door.

I made myself a sandwich too. It seemed quite natural now to bring a tray up to his room and balance it on the bed while I cleared the bedside table and drew up a chair. All the same, I said,

"Do you mind if I eat here too?"

"Not at all," he said mildly. "I'm dying for a cup of tea."

"Poor you. What did you do before, when you were sick?"

He made a non-committal gesture, and we ate in silence for a while.

"What are you doing this evening?"

"No plans. Are you up to backgammon? Or do you just want to sleep?"

I hoped he would say no, and we could play. Backgammon was a perfect background for a talk. He sighed. "Maybe not backgammon," he said.

"Ok. Can I do anything else?"

He seemed to hesitate. "Would you read to me?"

"Of course!" I was delighted. I washed up, and then rummaged in the back room and climbed the stairs with an armload of books.

"I hope you're planning to be sick for at least a week," I said, nudging open his door.

"Oh my goodness!" he said, and then he patted the

bed beside him. "Let's see what you've got. Where are my glasses."

We chose short stories, because Hugh said his attention span wasn't very long.

"I'll have some of these," he said, laying aside an old tatty Grimms Fairytales, and then he picked out another book. "And there's a story in here I want to hear again. I think you'll like it."

He settled back and I began to read. We had King Grisly-Beard first. Then The Lady and the Lion. Hugh told me I read well. Rene and I read to each other frequently, I said. We'd read the whole of The Gormenghast Trilogy aloud. Had he any requests? He chose The King of the Golden Mountain. After a few more tales, his eyes were closed and he was breathing deeply. But when I laid the book aside, he opened his eyes.

"I'm not asleep. How about that John Cheever story." I said ok, but first a hot drink. I made us cocoa and persuaded Hugh to choke down a chocolate biscuit or two.

"Tomorrow it's spinach and oxtail soup," I warned him and he grimaced.

"I think you'll have to write me a sick note Monday."

I thought of my own Monday morning, typing up reports. John was right. It was as if I'd been leaving all along, and London was a stopover. I glanced down at the globe, then lifted it onto my lap. Australia. The Coral Sea. Arafura, Timor, Tasman. I had never seriously studied the continent before. A cold feeling crept in the pit of my stomach. All that way?

"Hugh," I said.

"Yes?"

Then I thought, no. Think about it more. Once it's in words, you'll go, or you'll regret staying.

"John had a strange attitude to going."

"You mean his finality?"

"Not only that. It's as though he...I don't know, it sounds, weird, but it's almost as though he wanted everything to cease to exist as soon as he left."

"Yes. I can understand that. Did he want you to cease too?"

141

I smiled. "He said I was sleeping."

Hugh raised his eyebrows. "Sleeping."

"D'you want that story?"

"Page seven hundred and thirteen."

The story was about a man who is swimming in a friend's pool and gets the idea he can swim the eight miles to his home through all his friends' pools. But time leaves the man behind: his friends become increasingly cool to him as he swims; his mistress is rude. As his strength diminishes, his bewilderment grows. When he reaches his own home it is locked and empty and he cries for the first time in his adult life.

I put the book down and we were both quiet for a while. I wondered if Hugh was asleep this time and I studied his face, and his hands, folded on the covers. The fingers were fat. He wore no rings. His nails were perfect pale crescents. Funny that daddy's hands were so slender. Daddy's hands and Rene's hands. Hugh opened his eyes.

"Will you go to Australia?"

I was momentarily robbed of words. He studied me calmly, no trace of emotion, the perfect poker face.

"Yes."

"Have you told your dad?"

"I've only just...told myself."

He nodded, then his eyes fell on the globe at the foot of the bed.

"All that way," he said. "I suppose I shall have to come and visit. The pity is, I have a horror of long flights."

"Oh I shan't fly."

"No?"

"No." I studied my outstretched fingers, and the way the skin over the knuckles was puckered, like cellophane when you stretch it a little and then let it go. "I'll swim."

The Test

no motion has she now, no force
she neither hears nor sees
rolls round in earth's diurnal course
with rocks and stones and trees

6pm Tuesday.

I wouldn't have started in this colour of fear, but every evening around now – five, six, seven – it gets dark like this. Big storm clouds mass up and yesterday a bolt of lightning forked down like a snake's tongue and bit into the scaffolding outside. I ran into the hallway and put on a pair of rubber-soled shoes and felt how my heart was banging.

"My heart is really banging!" I said aloud, experimentally, and it was a little calming to hear the words in my own voice. At the same time the skin under my arms prickled unpleasantly and I felt hot and weak.

I got courage washing, climbing those wooden steps to the laundry room. Only a couple of weeks ago the heat up there was red, but last night we were cold. The sun went down astonishingly, angrily. We began to feel the awful quiet dark, gathering in the flat.

"Let's go to Lola's party," I said, not believing we would.

"Alright. Let's." Al said, and we both got our coats at once, because to hesitate would mean sitting in the dark until it was time to go to bed.

The party was a strange animal; my old friends didn't seem to want to know me any more, and I didn't want to go in where there was dancing, and it was cold. In bed later, my feet would not warm up. Al slept, his arm flung across the sheet. He was frightened.

At two in the morning, a man was shouting drunk in the car park. All down the street he flickered in and out of peoples' dreams. Sleep pawed blindly at my window and into the room the man stumbled, holding a green glass bottle and shouting out the test results. "Oh no" I mumbled, coming half awake at the same time, "it's my fault..." On and on he was shouting, a litany of medical terms. I couldn't quite hear them but I knew what they were and I twisted in the bed to make him stop. Even then, when I was fully awake, and the strips of light were as they were every night on the bedroom wall, I felt I knew without question what the man had been shouting.

I dragged myself up in the bed until I could see over the windowsill. It took me a while to make him out, sitting on a curb with his legs spread out in front of him and a white singlet on. Was he only wearing a singlet in the night? I felt suddenly sick with shame, lying there watching him, hiding below the window ledge. I slid back down in the bed. The quilt was too heavy now. "Don't leave!" the man shouted. They were too clear, the words. I watched the clock until it was nearly three.

This morning we sat in the sittingroom and could not leave. There are days like that: they will not begin. Some band was singing on the radio, 'I don't know why sometimes I get frigh-tened'. Al was terribly quiet. Then a Beatles song. They play three or four in an hour, the oldest songs, full of Sunday mornings when I was a kid. What's wrong with remembering? On Christmas morning we had to wait for the grandmothers to come back from church in fur coats. Then we could open the presents.

"Come on," Al said in the end. "Let's go."

Walking round the lake, the sunshine was stiff and the clouds very high up and innocent. By five they would be like this, towering and jealous.

At the station we saw a blind man who was lost. He was banging into things with his stick and shouting "I'm blind and I need some help." At first, we held back, wanting to avoid it, the naked white stick. Blind people always seem so capable. They tap the wall, they stop at curbs, they pause to get their bearings, then go on. No one ever shouted for help like this before. Then we both felt ashamed at the same time and started forward. The man clung to my arm while we led him down to the trains. He said hardly anything but held on and I thought "I will be able to feel his hand gripping my arm long after he has gone." He talked a little but he seemed gruff and I was impatient and ashamed and sorry. I could hardly make my brain think about being blind. It was more like repeating in fear "I don't want to be blind! I don't want to be blind!" and without transition I was telling myself I did not want to die.

1pm Wednesday

I found I had written words without even hearing what the lecturer said. I was high up in one of the larger theatres. The gradient was vertiginous. I crept in late and sat shaking at the back, trying to slip into the atmosphere of the class, the casual attention, feet on the chairbacks, occasional notes. Then a dream of last night blossomed in my head and I sat very still, trying to recapture the emotional atmosphere that coloured the dream, that seemed strangely separate from what went on. I was up at night looking after my grandfather and we both knew, sort of amusedly, that he was going to die. When the time came, he stood up and he was in my arms at a shelf or desk, and then *I* was in someone's arms and I was doing the dying and I hoped it would be over quickly without any great pain at the heart. I was ready, and then it came and it was over and I was just sort of calm. I laid him out and left the room to wake my parents and tell them it was done.

Dante, I had written. Halfway through my life I woke up in a dark forest. Virgil guides him through the Inferno and Purgatory, and Beatrice brings him to Paradise. Virgil his favourite poet. Beatrice his love. Who will guide me through the Inferno? Gertrude Stein wrote a poem that went something like: "yes yes yes yes yes yes you bet yes certainly yes yes no." The Frosts

145

had five children but lost one. *No motion has she now, no force, she neither hears nor sees...*

I was writing the words as I heard them, in a kind of panic. It was so lonely, sitting there, all of life just coming and going, coming and going, sleeping and waking.

"That's what poetry is – it's a twin flower – tries to say both things at the same time."

I looked up from my frantic scribbling. People were sitting with their eyes closed. There were the usual huddles of two, whispering, a hand on a girl's back, moving up and down the cotton. I got up in a hurry and left. It was over anyway. Two hours to go now. Halfway through my life I woke up in a dark forest.

2pm Wednesday

I ate no lunch again. For the second day I queued in two different sandwich bars and watched with a growing nausea as people ordered sandwiches and picked apples or chocolate bars. Just short of the counter I felt light-headed, the pounding started and I turned away. I sat on the grass between attempts to buy some lunch, until there was no point any longer. There were disconnected phrases from the lecture in my head, and names that hung together in bunches: the late Victorians, the Modernists, the pre Raphaelites. "What shall we do," I murmured and got up to walk. Three o'clock, they said. It is scarcely two. The hospital is up at the north end of the campus. You cling on to your health hungrily in a hospital and you want to be seen to be carrying the flowers. The place smells of fear: there *is* such a smell. Dogs catch it, and rabbits give it off. I would try to write to my mother but it would make me cry and I would have to give up. You know that feeling after you've cried a lot: like a beach after heavy waves. Flotsam and jetsam. Al and I in the water on a Greek beach last summer: "I'm Flotsam." "Hi Flotsam! I'm Jetsam!"

2.30pm Wednesday

I passed the cool green slope where I often lie reading, watching a football game, with the sounds of water from the swimming pool. It would be nice to lie face down in the dark grass, but I cannot sleep or lie down. I am vertical, like Sylvia Plath. I thought of her with her two kids in a flat on Primrose Hill. I don't know if I was more scared on my own, when it was just me who knew, or after I told Al. He got terribly quiet and still. Then it was a reality, it had come out in words. But I have not written it down. I have not written it down. Some time the point comes where childhood must stop and you can never look back in the same way as you did. You wish for it to be the same as it was; it was warm and comfortable, it was dull, and even that seems enviable. It can never be the same. Look forward. Carry out the simple tasks – put the washing in the dryer and keep vertical.

Nothing is quite normal. O God, *purifiez nos coeurs.* I'm going now.

Friday the first.

A new month and I hope we always remember Wednesday as the day the scare lifted oh I hope we never forget that date for that and what a scare I wouldn't have had it happen that way but the tests showed negative and Al was laughing on the phone when I said it's all alright Al and we came quickly out of the fright and we are out the other side and in clear air and sunshine and we shiver and laugh with relief and I know this is a hopelessly long sentence but that is just what life is going to be from now on just a long sentence with no punctuation until the full stop at the end.

Thin Ice

Perhaps, at eleven, it was Christopher I feared most in the world, and I suspect that, at forty-two, he feared me. That Christmas we went down to grandfather's in Sussex. The south of England sat patiently under heavy snow. The beach looked odd beside snow, and the dogs loved it, rushing through the woods, setting off small avalanches from the still branches with their barking. Ian said, as he saw the ice begin to thaw between myself and my new father:

"Good. Let it all be over now. Let the two of you be friends."

Ian chose his words carefully. He steered away from words that would topple me into a mute resistance as skillfully as he drew the dogs away from the ice.

I was learning a lot of things that Christmas, but I thought I already knew a great deal. I knew there was a god who had my death written down on his calendar, and who knew when it would happen and, more importantly, how. I knew it wouldn't be for a long time: not, say, until after I was seventeen and had been to a disco. It could be lung cancer, I reckoned, because Frank Keily had taught me to smoke cigarettes in the henhouse in his father's garden – how to hold them and suck in carefully so you didn't cough up and set off a cloud of chicken feathers. God was very real to me then. I thought he needed a lot more space than most people seemed to give him. Ian thought so too and when he found me clearing all the surfaces in my bedroom he knew I was making space and he left me alone. He did not point out, like Christopher did, that having your books and pencils and photograph albums all in the wardrobe when there were perfectly good shelves made

149

no sense. I cannot say whether I was scared of the man my mother had married because he was only learning to be a father and I knew it, or whether it was because he shouted and sometimes broke things, when he was angry. I know I began to like him the day he brought his hand down on a vase that had been my grandmother's and cracked it so he cut his finger badly and had to sit in silence while my mother dressed it. That day I realised that you could be grown up and still do things you had to suffer for. Still, the streak of restless resentment in me caused me to say the kind of things that provoked him into these rages. It was long after this day that I first allowed feelings of affection, even of acceptance, to be admitted. Before this happened there had to be a lot of shouting and a lot of bringing down of hands. They even tried to send me away to school, but I could not sleep in a room that was not next to the room where Ian slept and I only stayed in that school for a week. My mother took me home then because I was ill.

In grandfather's house there was a piano. We had no piano where we lived in London but some of my friends had pianos and I knew that Virginia Cole had first kissed a boy under a piano. It was at a birthday party, but nobody ever explained to me that there were two different types of piano – one that stood up and one that lay sort of propped on its elbow. My grandfather's piano stood up and I stared at it for a long time wondering how Virginia got all that kissing done in such a small space. She was a very active girl and I knew kissing involved quite a bit of moving about.

The day after Christmas I climbed a tree to see how far off France was. People said it wasn't too far off the coast of England and if they dug a tunnel under the channel you could make a train get there in less than an hour. I couldn't see it and, in the most petulant moment of my disappointment, I misjudged how high off the ground a branch can be when it has taken you four different footholds to get to it. I suppose it was jumping out of that tree that really ensured a lifelong friendship with my new father; but at that moment, the awful sickening jarring moment when I realised that I had landed on my feet but they had slipped from under me, I simply screamed as any hurt eleven-year-old would have. Something inside me that hadn't wanted to come apart was forced to do so and I could only think through all that pain of Katy in *What Katy Did*, who had fallen off a swing and hurt her back and how, for some reason I couldn't recall, she had to cook the dinner for her whole family for a long time. When Christopher found me, all the tears were gone and I was crying a dryness that hurt my throat even more than it hurt my back. I had to let the pain do anything it wanted. I had to sob in arid croaks into Christopher's shoulder all the way back up to the house, and I couldn't help repeating over and over "I don't want to cook the dinner! Don't make me cook the dinner!". In spite of this, there was still part of my mind that bitterly resented being caught sobbing like a baby. So I was mildly surprised when, through the fog of being undressed and put to bed, I heard Christopher explaining reasonably that Katy only had to *decide* what everyone should have for dinner, and tell the cook; and this was because her mummy was dead, so she had to act mummy; and even though I still had a mummy, who was perfectly alive and loved me very much, I could, if I wished, decide what everyone should have for dinner for as long as I liked, and he would try and make sure they got it.

After I had lain in bed for a bit and Christopher had phoned the doctor and the friends whom my mother and Ian and grandfather were visiting, he came and sat on the bed and held my hand and I felt the bandage on his finger and pretty soon I forgot that he had married my mother to try and make a stranger of her, and I remembered instead how still and quietly he had sat while she was bandaging the finger. Suddenly it seemed clear to me that if I was frightened of him, he might also be frightened of me, and since the pain in my back was making spots before my eyes, I let a fresh wave of tears carry me into a jumble of murmured confessions to which he listened with a grave, but not unkind expression on his face. When he thought I was asleep he smoothed the covers a little and just before he turned the light out I felt his lips brush softly against my hair.

I woke from a sullen, heavy sleep and the room was lit by a green lamp, spreading light like a pale, watery, green sun.

"You fell. You hurt your back," my mother told me firmly. "Does it still hurt?"

Ian was there, and when I tried to sit up and fell back with a louder cry than was really necessary, he winced. Ian felt other peoples' pain as though his own was not enough. Christopher was not in the room.

"Who made the light green?"

"We've put green lenses in your eyes," Ian said. "Look at me, I'm G-R-E-E-N!" he leered over the bed, and then ruffled my hair. "Who told you the ground was bouncy?"

"I didn't bounce," I muttered thickly, caught between a laugh and tears. I was exploring the possibilities of the occasion. My mother moved about the room, doing things I couldn't see.

"Can we have jam doughnuts for dinner?" I said. "And clam soup?"

She stopped. "Together? Or separately? Or perhaps you'd like clam doughnuts and jam soup?" she smiled. "Go ahead. Tell us what we'll have for dinner. It saves your grandfather a lot of trouble."

I ordered mushroom omelette and peanut butter, doughnuts and ribena. Everyone had to drink ribena, from the plastic tumblers we used on the beach in the summer for picnics. Later in the evening I asked for paper and a pencil and wrote down a painful list of my favourite foods.

"How d'you spell chocolate mousse? How d'you spell toasted cheese sandwiches with pickle and tomato ketchup?"

And the next day while mother was shopping and grandfather had taken Ian out with the dogs, I told Christopher that the only way I could really be at peace would be if my bed were brought into the library. I even used that phrase, 'at peace'. Somewhere in my head I had a picture of being laid out in the library, the white sheet turned back and my hands folded restfully over it. There would be a slight smile on my face and when the people saw me, they would cry, with white handkerchiefs, and murmur 'at peace'.

Christopher moved my bed. The library was down a narrow polished landing from my room. It was filled with an accumulation – forty, fifty years of books, maps, models, glass, bits and pieces. It was a wealthy room. Astronomical instruments of brass and models of bronze stood on the shelves; books lined the walls, floor to ceiling. A figure of a woman hung poised from the ceiling and grandfather had once had to point out to me how one of her feet was attached to a solid wood bookmark on the top shelf. And there were photographs, black-and-white ones, pictures of the serious, lovely girl who was my grandmother: looking downwards out of a window, wearing a broad-brimmed hat, the lack of colour highlighting the structure of her face.

"I knew a woman lovely in her bones," murmured Christopher. He was looking at the photographs while I was clambering slowly into my bed and he did not know whether to go or to stay. It seemed to be very awkward for him. I had had a dream of him before I woke to the green light, and after this dream I thought a lot more of how he had brought me in his arms back to the house, and of how he had looked as he put me on the bed, and of his bandaged finger – and I wondered if it hurt him.

"You can tell me a story if you like." My voice surprised even myself when it came out. I had meant to say it nicely. It came out like a bark.

"I don't know stories." He kept looking at the photographs.

"Well...tell me...tell me about times you were in foreign places then."

"In where?"

"Spain" I said promptly, sensing the bait taken.

Christopher was not very used to telling stories. You could see it sat ill with him, to settle into a story-telling frame of mind, even to find the correct position on the side of my bed. I was afraid to help him out, to make even the smallest gesture that might indicate I was no longer feeling exactly the way I had been feeling towards him. I didn't snuggle down a little in the bed and assume an expression of dreamy attention. I didn't give a funny sigh that would indicate I was all settled down and ready for some stories. I didn't put my hand down near his. I thought of doing it, and it sent a shiver over me.

"Once," he began, and paused so long I became aware of every breath I took, "I saw a man get on a trolley bus with no money. When the conductor came to him he explained he had no money, and he offered to write a note promising to pay the money to the trolley bus company."

"Was he poor? Did he wear raggedy clothes?"

"No. No – he was quite well dressed. He wrote the note carefully on a page of his notebook with a fountain pen. And the conductor took it and folded it and put it in his breast pocket. And that was that."

"Wasn't it all jiggling in the bus? I mean, how could he write?"

"I expect," Christopher answered gravely, "it was pretty difficult to write in a trolleybus, yes."

"And...and why didn't everyone else try the same thing?"

"I don't know. But nobody did."

I thought for a while about the man sitting on the trolleybus, writing out this note with his fountain pen and Christopher thought about it too. After a while I said:

"Are there any more stories?"

My voice sounded very small in the room full of books and maps and astrological instruments. Christopher thought some more.

"There was once a room," he said at last, "that was thirty feet across and circular. The ceiling was made of stone and if a person stood against the wall and whispered very quietly, close into the wall, another person standing on the other side of the room, if he put his ear very close up to his bit of wall, could hear the whisper. Clear as if it were right – in – his – ear."

I rolled this story round my mouth for a little and

when I had got my tongue around it I asked:

"What would the person whisper?" with a sense as I said it of the stories ending.

"He would whisper," Christopher said slowly and bent down close to my ear, "sleep now and dream sweetly."

There was a lot of trouble about my move to the library, but I stayed there for a week until I was well, inventing menus and reading the titles of the books as far as I could make them out from my bed. Ian entertained me a great deal and in the evenings I was allowed downstairs to sit by the fire in the sitting room; but during the mornings when everyone was out, Christopher would come and sit by my bed. Sometimes he would read his paper or smoke a pipe. Sometimes he told me stories about Spain or about the time he lived in Africa. Sometimes he just sat in silence. My mother protested about draughts and about the inconvenience; my grandfather plodded in and out, fetching books and carrying them downstairs to read in the kitchen porch. My mother said you couldn't sleep in a library; she said you read in a library, that there was no room there for beds, that that was what bedrooms were for. She pointed out to Christopher the marks made by dragging the bed on the polished wooden floor of the landing and she wondered aloud what on earth he had been thinking of. Christopher would wink at me and keep quiet. I don't think he ever told my mother just what he had been thinking of.